Friction

Also by E. R. Frank

America

Dime

Life Is Funny

Wrecked

Friction

E. R. FRANK

A Richard Jackson Book
Atheneum Books for Young Readers
NEW YORK LONDON TORONTO SYDNEY NEW DELHI

ATHENEUM BOOKS FOR YOUNG READERS • An imprint of Simon & Schuster Children's Publishing Division • 1230 Avenue of the Americas, New York, New York 10020 •

• Interior design by Mike Rosamilia; cover design and hand-lettering by Russell Gordon • The text for this book is set in Hoefler. • Manufactured in the United States of America • First Atheneum Books for Young Readers paperback edition May 2015 • 1 2 3 4 5 6 7 8 9 10 • The Library of Congress has cataloged the hardcover edition as follows: • Frank. E. R. • Friction / E. R. Frank. • p. cm. • "A Richard Jackson book." • Summary: When a new girl at the private school Alex attends starts rumors about Alex's favorite teacher, Alex and her eighth-grade classmates are not sure how to act around him or with one another. • ISBN 978-0-689-85384-5 (hc) • [1. Teacher-student relationships—Fiction. 2. Child sexual abuse—Friction. 3. Coming of age—Friction.] I. Title. • PZ7.F84913 Fr 2003 • [Fic]—dc21 • 2002008040 • ISBN 978-1-4814-4810-9 (pbk) • ISBN 978-1-4391-1613-5 (eBook)

For all my teachers

1

THE FIRST TIME we all meet Stacy, it's just a regular morning.

Our teacher, Simon, is in front of the room, shuffling flash cards. He leans back against the science counter, mixes the deck a couple of times, and hooks one ankle over the other, the way he always does. Then he holds up the first word.

"Ology," he says out loud, so we can hear how it sounds. I write, *the study of.* Things are quiet while pencils scratch, sounding just like gerbils making a nest out of cedar chips and Kleenex. Simon holds up the next one. *Astro.* On a test he'll put them together, and we'll have to figure out that *astrology* means "the study of stars."

"Ichthy," Simon says. *Fish,* I write, and then I kick Tim and

make a gagging face to remind him how we remember that one: Fish tastes icky. . . . *ichthy*. But Tim doesn't kick back, even when I kick him again, and then I notice there's this massive hush in the room. I look up to see a girl standing in the doorway. The new girl. Simon told us she was coming, but up until this second I'd forgotten all about it.

She's got shiny black hair down to her behind and gray eyes that take up her whole face, and she's as skinny as I am. She's wearing a purple-and-black turtleneck and jeans that look brand-new, and she grins at everybody like she's totally psyched to meet us. She's got a gap between her two front teeth.

"Hi," she goes. "I'm Stacy." I see a flash of silver in her mouth. A tongue ring. "Let's get this party started."

And that's how it begins.

2

SIMON CLOSES HIS eyes, jabs his finger on the class list hanging over the science counter, and lands on *Alex.* So I get to show Stacy around.

"How old are you?" is the first thing she asks after Simon leaves us alone.

"Twelve," I say. "My birthday's not until August. But everybody else is thirteen."

"Huh." Stacy raises her black eyebrows. "So you must be really smart." She's kind of small, but something about the way she stands definitely seems older.

"Nah," I say, walking out of the front classroom into the side hallway to show her the bathrooms and our little kitchen. "I just started school young."

"So where's my class, then?" Stacy asks, walking with me.

"Where's all the fourteen-year-olds?" That must be her age. She must have gotten left back once.

"This is it," I say. I stop when we hit the back classroom. Stacy stops with me.

"After next year we're done. They don't teach past ninth grade at Forest Alternative."

"Where are all the ninth graders?" she asks, looking around.

"There aren't any yet," I explain. "We'll be the first ones. Simon will stay our teacher, and then after we leave, he'll start over with the new sixth graders."

"Weird," Stacy goes. She turns to weave through the classroom tables, and I follow her. When she gets to the glass wall, she leans forward to mush her nose right on it. "What's this room for?"

"It's the silent study room and Simon's office. You can go online anytime you want in there, only nobody's allowed to talk, except to Simon. If you do, you lose half an hour of game time on games day."

"What's games day?" Stacy looks through the glass at Simon, who's leaning over a couple of kids and a geometry book.

"We just get a break from our regular work. We get to play stuff like Scrabble and chess." Stacy moves back from the wall, lifts her long hair, and smoothes it across one shoulder so that it spills over onto her front.

"No offense," she says, "but this school is freaking weird."

"Yeah," I say. "I know."

"When my mom told me each grade has the same teacher all day long here, I thought I'd hate it." She's studying Simon. "But not anymore." She shakes her head, hair fanning out everywhere, all dramatic. "He is a total babe."

"Who?" I go. "Simon?"

"Mm-hmm," Stacy says, widening her eyes at me and heading for the glass door. "Don't you think he's hot?"

"I guess," I say, even though I never thought about it before, and then I follow her through the silent study room to the front classroom, where we started. The other kids pretend to concentrate on their work, but I see them checking us out, wondering what she's like.

"Where's he from?" Stacy asks, looking over at Viv.

"He's Indian," I say. "India Indian, not cowboys and." I've known Viv so long, I barely notice his vanilla swirl turban anymore.

"Wild," Stacy says, like she's impressed.

We pass Tim, who's asleep over a word problem, with *Rate x Time = Distance* scrawled on his paper. I snap him on the head, and Stacy grins when he shoots up like a rubber ball bouncing off pavement. I like her smile. That gap between her teeth looks perfect for spitting through. I bet she's a good aim, when she wants to be. Now she's tapping her tongue ring on her lower lip and trying not to stare.

"There's crippled kids here?" she whispers.

"That's Sebastian." His legs are twisted really bad, so he has to wear braces on them, and his arms end at the elbows, and he falls a lot and has to be helped up. Only you have to do it the way he likes, or else he'll yell at you, and he can be loud.

Stacy tucks her tongue back into her mouth. "Jesus," she whispers again, all serious. "That's got to suck."

"Yeah, but don't say that to him," I tell her. "He hates pity." I pull on her arm. "Come on. Outside is part of the tour."

I race out the double doors and hop over the short slate path leading to the lower school. Then I whip down and around the side of our building, dodging a couple of ice patches and leftover winter slush. While Stacy catches up to me at the bottom of the hill near the edge of the woods, I roll the sleeves of my blue sweater down over my hands to keep them warm. Stacy dives after me into the trees, toward the ladder and stream. Old branches snap under our feet, and the air chills the tips of my ears.

"At recess the girls come down here and build forts and stuff," I say as we slow to a stop. "I play soccer up on the field with most of the guys."

The stream is about four feet wide and trades off being shallow and deep in places, and it always flows fast. There's an old ladder here, lying across the two banks, making a bridge. Sometimes we all hang out by the ladder, practicing running across on the rungs. Once you get the hang of it, learn how to plant your feet and carry your weight just right, you don't even have to think. It's almost as good as juggling a soccer ball one hundred times in a row without messing up. "I want to play professionally when I'm older," I tell Stacy, running across the ladder, back, and across again. "You know. Like, for a living."

We haven't ever had a real coach with real practices because our school never had extra money for that stuff. But soon it won't matter. "Next fall Simon's going to coach us, and we'll get to compete in the private-school league." Tim and I can't wait. We want to be on the same teams all the time and get to travel around the world and maybe try out for the Olympics someday.

"But girls don't play in boys' leagues," Stacy goes. I run the ladder again, and she watches my feet hit the rungs.

"There aren't any girls in the boys' league right now, but

my parents say if I want to and I'm good enough, it's against the law to keep me off. So I'm just going to practice really hard and not worry about it."

I stop in the middle of the ladder, balancing over water on nothing but the balls of my feet and the metal bars. One teeter in either direction, and I could fall. "What about you?" I ask. "What do you want to do?" I hop my way to the opposite bank, surprised that Stacy doesn't answer right away. She seems like the type of person who has an answer for everything. But she just pulls her hands out of her coat and winds her hair around an arm, over her sleeve. She gets a thick coil from her shoulder to her elbow before she speaks.

"I want to be powerful and rich," she says. "But not famous." She keeps winding, and the coil thins out as it gets near her wrist. "I'll be in the CIA," she says. "Nobody can find you that way, unless you want them to." Stacy smiles a little and heads for the ladder. "Hey"—she slides her right foot onto the right solid edge of the metal and then does the same with her left and the left edge—"is that blond guy your boyfriend?" She glides out a little bit, keeping the edges centered lengthwise under her feet.

"That's Tim," I say. "He's my best friend." Stacy makes her way across the ladder to me. "His mom sometimes works at the same clinic as my parents. They're doctors. She's a nurse." Stacy steps carefully onto the bank.

"What's his dad do?" she asks. She stands closer to you than most people. I can feel her breath on my face.

"He runs a taxi service." I turn to walk along the stream, in the opposite direction from the school building.

"What kind of doctor is your dad?" Stacy goes. I grab a couple of small rocks from the ground and start chucking them across the stream. I'm not aiming at any one thing, but I keep hitting the same branch anyway.

"Psychiatrist," I say. "You know. He talks to people about their problems and gives them medicine to not be depressed and things like that."

Stacy throws a couple of rocks too before we turn around to head back. We're quiet for awhile, so all we hear is the grinding of our feet on cold ground and the spilling sound of the stream. Just when we can see the ladder again, Stacy goes, "My father's dead."

I stop in my tracks. She steps close, the tips of her shoes practically touching mine. Her voice gets low, and she looks me straight in the eye.

"He was in a car wreck," she says. "He would have been okay, but the thing is, we're Jehovah's Witnesses, and we can't have blood transfusions because they interfere with the will of the Lord." At first I think she might be kidding, because nothing about her seems like she could talk about the "will of the Lord" in such a serious way. But who would joke about their father being dead? I know what transfusions are. That's when you've bled so much that the hospital has to give you other blood that goes from plastic bags through tubes into your veins.

"What's a Jehovah's Witness?" I ask, but it comes out all wrong, like I'm starting to tell a joke or something.

"It's a religion," Stacy says. "It has a lot of rules. Like you can't celebrate birthdays or Halloween. There's all this stuff about what you can and can't do, especially if you're sick or hurt or something."

"It doesn't seem very fair," I go. Then I bite my lip. It's bad enough her father died. I shouldn't make it worse by insulting her religion.

"Don't tell anybody," she goes.

"Why not?"

She shrugs and kicks at the ground. A rock loosens under her sneaker and rolls away, leaving a small hole in the icy soil. She dips her head, and her hair falls over her face like a dark curtain.

"I don't want anyone knowing about it. I don't like to talk about it. I had to leave my other school because everybody kept wanting to ask me questions all the time. I can't stand questions like that."

Stacy rushes past me toward the ladder. She slides across it fast and then runs up the hill, only she turns the wrong way on the slate path and goes through the wrong double doors, right inside the lower school. I follow her, fast. She gets all the way to the painted mural wall a bunch of us made a few years ago before she stops and turns around. "I only told you because you're someone I can trust," she says, crossing her arms and then crossing them the other way. She's standing in front of my part of the mural: a girl kicking a soccer ball. One leg looks like a bat, and the hair looks like a bell. I'm a crappy artist. "I can trust you, can't I?" Stacy says, crossing her arms the other way, for the millionth time. I only wait for a second, thinking about how hard it will be not telling Tim, or Simon, about Stacy's father. Especially Tim. I tell him everything.

"You can trust me," I finally say. Because when people tell you a secret, it's like a gift. You don't just give it away to someone else, even if you never asked for it in the first place.

3

"NO OFFENSE," I hear Teddy saying when we're getting ready for lunch, "but I can't help you, buddy." Besides being really fat, Teddy's a vocabulary genius. Plus, he's beaten the college kids at the city math contest two years in a row.

"Come on, man," Danny's begging. "I don't understand that tenths crap." Danny's got blue hair, and he sucks at math. He follows Teddy over to the rectangular table. I grab my brown bag and watch Stacy, who's leaning against the lockers.

"Actually," Teddy goes, "it's tens, not ten*ths*."

"Decimals," Sebastian says to Danny, bumping himself into a seat. "Not fractions, you idget." Danny flips him the finger, and Stacy glances my way and cracks a smile. The gap in her teeth winks at me.

Simon looks at her. "You doing okay?" I hear him ask.

"Yeah," Stacy says. "I'm good."

I step over and grab her arm. "Sit here."

Tim plops down next to us at the square table.

"You forgot your lunch?" he goes to Stacy as she pulls some wrinkled bills out of her back pocket.

"Where's the cafeteria?"

"We don't have one," Tim says. He takes a stack of green papers from Danny, pulls us each a sheet, and then hands off the pile to Viv at the next table.

"Wild," Stacy goes. "No bells, no gym, no cafeteria." I hand her half my sandwich, and she takes it without missing a beat. "Totally wild." She bites into the bread. "Thanks," she goes, after she swallows. "I owe you."

Tim glances at her, trying to figure her out, I guess, like I've been doing all morning. It's hard not being allowed to tell him her secret.

"Okay, guys." Simon claps his hands together twice. He's standing in the middle of the room, turning his head in every direction so we can all hear. "The green paper has some reminders for your parents on the camping trip which, FYI, is in less than two weeks." He hands a stack of yellow papers to Teddy, who takes one and passes the rest around. "The yellow paper is the permission slip and medical form for the fall soccer league." Simon unwraps a tuna sandwich from a piece of plastic wrap that he saves and reuses all the time. "I know next fall seems like it's far away, but I need these back ASAP."

"Hey, Simon," Danny says, "are we going to get to play any public schools next year? My cousin's on Lincoln's team, and I want to kick his butt."

"It's a private-school league," Marie goes, as if Danny's stupid or something—which he sort of is sometimes, but she doesn't have to be such a priss about it.

Simon ignores Marie. "No, Danny," he goes. "Private schools play private schools. Public schools play public."

"I'd have to go to Lincoln with Danny's cousin next year if I didn't go here," Tim says. I would too. Lincoln's the only public school in my district. And except for Forest Alternative, my parents don't really like the private schools around here. Tim called my mom a "reverse snob" once, and he's probably right.

"Lots of public schools are decent," Stacy says loudly. "Like Clearview and Rockwell. But Lincoln sucks."

"Yeah?" Danny goes, dragging a chair over to our table. "How do you know?"

"I just came from there, Goldilocks," Stacy answers, tilting her head at him like she thinks he's cute. Danny smiles and runs his hand through his hair. Blue looks good on him, and he knows it. Stacy keeps talking. "Lincoln's got hundreds of kids, and only the special-ed ones have the same teacher all day. The bathrooms are just stalls with no doors, and half the time the toilets are stopped up." Tim shoves one of his peanut butter crackers toward her. "Thanks," she goes, and then she nods at Teddy. "I hate to say it, but kids like you get beat up all the time."

"Really?" He squints at her. "For what?"

Stacy starts pressing numbers on her calculator watch. "What's one hundred and eight times four hundred and sixty-four divided by point five?" She punches all the buttons as fast as she talks. I guess she saw Teddy in action earlier.

"One hundred thousand two hundred and twenty-four," Teddy goes.

Stacy glances at her wrist. "Wow."

The rest of us are quiet for a minute.

"Besides," Sebastian finally says to Teddy, "you're fat." Teddy goes pink. "Relax," Sebastian tells him. Then he turns to Stacy. "They'd crucify me at Lincoln, right?" He means because he's crippled. Challenged. Whatever.

Stacy leans her chair back onto its hind legs and balances there. "Truthfully?" Her tongue ring flashes at us. "They'd make you ride a different bus and put you in the same room with all the special-ed kids all day." She brings her chair back to the floor with a thump and lets out a big sigh. "Punks," she says quiet to Sebastian. He shrugs and then stares at his nubby elbows. The rest of us stare anywhere but at him.

"Are any of the teachers like Simon?" Tim asks.

Stacy sighs again. "You'd never call Lincoln teachers by their first names," she goes. "They're almost as bad as the kids. The kids there are a bunch of idiots." She tilts her head at all of us this time. "You guys are a lot cooler." A compliment from Stacy seems like a big deal somehow. Even Danny looks shy all of a sudden.

He pushes his chair back, crumples up his lunch bag, and hooks it into the garbage can. "Last one to the net is second pick," he yells, and he's out the door.

"Hey, no fair," Tim goes, bolting out of his chair.

"See you later," I say to Stacy, and I'm gone.

Our soccer field isn't so great, even compared to Lincoln's, which isn't any big deal, either. But at least Lincoln's has grass and actual goalposts. Our field at Forest Alternative is mostly dirt, full of holes, and a total mud bath when it rains. We don't have posts, much less real nets, so we use jackets or logs to mark our goals. Still, it's better than playing on the blacktop, which we had to do until a couple of years ago, before they bulldozed a better space for us—one that wouldn't have cars coming and going all the time.

Tim and I end up on the same team, and it feels good to kick and pass with him. It feels good to forget about stuff like decimals and new girls and dead fathers and schools where everybody's a punk. It feels good to have nothing but sweaty bodies and voices calling back and forth, like chimes in the wind.

4

TIM SHOWS UP at my house just before my parents do. I was going to make hamburgers, but Tim wants pasta.

"How'd it go?" I ask. Tim's oral report on rappelling is coming up in a few days, and Simon's been helping him practice lowering himself off the school roof with special ropes and tools and things so that when it's time, Tim can demonstrate his topic besides just lecturing about it.

"Good." He pulls out a package of spaghetti from one of our kitchen cabinets. "We practiced knots and the right way to fall."

"I bet the new girl will want to try it on the camping trip. She's not going to be scared at all."

"Maybe." He brushes past me to the hanging rack of pots and pans, grabs a pot, and fills it with water. He's eaten dinner with us so many times, he knows the whole routine.

"I like her," I say, watching him slap a cover on the pot. "Don't you?"

He shrugs, and we hear my parents' car breathe into the garage and then burp to a stop.

"Hi, Tim," my dad goes, banging into the kitchen. "Your parents got the night shift again?"

"Yeah," Tim says. He sleeps over a lot when his parents have to work nights, which is kind of different since most kids our age don't have sleepovers with friends of the opposite sex. But Tim and I used to take baths together when we were babies and stuff. We're like a brother and a sister. So it's no big deal.

"No problem," my dad goes, nodding his head and making his orange hair flop around. "Alex's extra bed is still made up from last time."

"Hi, guys," my mother goes, walking into the kitchen and opening her mail at the same time. She's a general practitioner with a subspecialty in oncology, which means she treats a lot of people with cancer. When people meet my mom for the first time, they stare, especially men. I think that's because she's so pretty, with silver hair and a young face, and the two aren't supposed to go together, but on my mother they do.

"We got a new girl today," I tell her.

"Really?" My mom looks up from her mail. "How is she?"

"We like her," I go. "Right, Tim?"

"She knows kids who smoke," Tim says.

My mom passes off the mail to my father. "Lovely," she goes.

While my dad and Tim clear the dishes after dinner, I pull out Simon's permission slips. My mother fills out the soccer one first, and then she scans the green camping page.

"One parent chaperone," she says to my dad. "Do you think that's enough adults to supervise the rappelling?"

"Not to mention supervising everything else," my dad goes.

"It's plenty," I say. "Simon's really careful, and Teddy's father went with us last year, so he knows all the safety stuff."

"Simon wouldn't be able to do this at any other school," my mother says. "Not these days. Maggie's really something to be going along with it." Maggie's our principal.

"What do you mean?" Tim goes.

"You can't teach kids any which way anymore," my mom says. "Teachers and schools are a lot more accountable for things than they used to be. Simon's teaching the way people did thirty years ago, and I'm not sure his style is workable anymore."

"Huh?" Tim goes.

"Ann's talking about liability," my dad explains, as if Tim and I are supposed to understand what he's saying.

"And I'm talking about judgment," my mother says.

"Simon has good judgment," I go.

My mother glances at her watch and then at my dad. "Jack, we're going to be late." He picks up her arm and looks at her watch too. They have some board meeting tonight.

"Okay," he tells her. Then he turns to Tim and me. "Don't worry about the rest of the dishes, guys," he tells us. "We'll see you two in the morning."

They kiss the tops of our heads before they go.

Tim and I watch HBO until the garage comes alive again a few hours later, and then we jump into my twin beds, pretending to be asleep. We breathe deep and heavy and kind of loud. To be safe, Tim whispers ten *Mississippis* after my parents tiptoe away from my bedroom door, and then we throw off our covers. He drags the rocking chair from near my window, and I lift my desk stool, and we plunk them next to our beds. Then we drape our comforters to make a tent. Tim crawls in with the blankets and pillows, and I follow with a flashlight. Once we're all set up, we throw shadow shapes on the flimsy ceiling with our hands and the beam of light.

* * *

The next morning we jog from my back door down through the sloped woods toward Maple Avenue below. Our feet whomp down the trail, knapsacks swinging across our backs, branches flicking at our cheeks.

"Hole," Tim warns, which means there's a new sunken spot on the ground. Those spots trip us up a lot in the last days of March, right between winter and spring. He hops over it, and I hop too. Then I take the lead. Something tickles my face, and I duck.

"Spiderweb," I go, wiping at the air, and I hear Tim duck behind me.

As we get near the bottom of the woods, our soles slapping against the path, Tim says, "Last night, after dinner, were your parents trying to say that Simon isn't responsible or something?"

"Yeah," I go. "Isn't that dumb?"

"Your parents are nuts," Tim goes.

"Totally."

5

HIS BIKE IS already hanging from the ceiling, like some outer-space bug, and Simon's standing over a small flame. His coffee mug steams next to today's paper while the laptop is booting up next to that.

"What's the candle for?" I ask, unbuttoning my blue sweater as Tim and I walk into the silent study room. Simon snaps closed a lighter and stares at a white candle in a baked clay holder.

"It's for my brother," Simon says. I push aside some papers and make a seat for myself on the edge of his desk. Tim leans over to touch the clay holder.

"I didn't know you had a brother," I say.

"He died." Simon passes his pinky through the flame.

"When?" Tim asks.

"Five years ago today."

Tim crosses his arms, and I cup my hand over the mouth of Simon's coffee mug, feeling the steam wet my palm.

"Was he a teacher too?" I say.

"Most people wouldn't know it," he tells us after a minute, "but he was a teacher. In a way." We stay quiet, but Simon keeps going. "Andrew was older than me."

"Than I," Tim mumbles automatically.

"And he was a rebel. Got us both into all kinds of trouble."

"You used to get into trouble?" I say. I can't imagine Simon being a bad kid.

"I'll just say," he adds, "we made our growing-up mistakes. The way all kids are bound to do. The way the two of you will. The way adults can't stand." He stops quickly right there. Then he goes on again. "This," he says, nodding at the flame, "is something I got from a Jewish friend. He told me about lighting candles on the anniversary of a death. As a way to remember someone who's died. To show you honor him."

"But you're not Jewish," Tim says.

"I'm not of any faith," Simon says. He passes his pinky through the fire another time. "Really, this isn't the right kind of candle. Jewish people use a special one."

"Are you even allowed to do that?" Tim asks. "Change the way it's supposed to be?"

"As long as I'm respectful," Simon tells us.

"It's nice," I say. The flame looks like a little life to me. Like a small body, dodging and dancing.

"How was your brother a teacher?" Tim asks. Simon leans back in his chair, laces his fingers behind his head, and thunks his feet up on the desk.

"I was about your age," he begins. "Twelve. Maybe thirteen. Andrew must have been eighteen or nineteen." He shakes his head. "Took me out with him on a day trip. Way out into the country. Told me he was going to teach me something I'd never forget. I had no idea what it would be, but I followed him up this mountain, hoping for all kinds of things. Stupid things, really: dead bodies, gold bricks, a hidden cave. Stuff like that." Simon stops to take a long sip of coffee. "Walked up that mountain for a few hours. So tired, I thought my heart was going to bust right through my skin and out my chest. Andrew wouldn't say a word—wouldn't answer my questions, wouldn't tell me anything. Only sound he'd make was this buzz thing he used to do. A sort of whistle and a hum at the same time."

Tim and I smile. "That's what you do," Tim tells Simon. "You make that exact sound!"

"Huh," Simon says. It's funny to me that he didn't know that about himself. "Anyway," he goes, "that's the only noise

Andrew was making. I was nearly nuts by the time we got to the top. He started pulling things out of his pack, and I was thinking whatever it was he had to show me must be in there. Maybe it was a gun. A voodoo doll or a cut-off finger. Who knows what. But all he pulled out was our lunch and a pocketknife to help us eat it. Told me to stop firing questions at him and to be patient. So I shut up and caught my breath. Thought I'd go crazy from the suspense."

"So what was it?" I ask.

Simon drags his feet off the desk and leans forward in his chair, bringing his face up close to me and Tim. "After we ate, Andrew stood up, threw his pack on his back, asked if I was ready. Then he just took off running down that mountain. I didn't understand what was going on. Sure didn't want to be left behind, so I took off after him. Guess I expected him to stop or at least slow down for me, but he kept going fast. I knew if I lost sight of him, I'd be in deep trouble. No trail, and I didn't know my way around mountains yet. So I raced down after my brother. No time to think, no time to be scared, no time for anything. All I knew was to keep breathing. Keep putting one foot in front of the other and don't lose sight of him for half a second. Not for branches in my face or the ground flying up at me. Once you start running down a mountain like that, there's no controlling it.

You can't just stop. You can't even slow down, really. All you can do is let the earth hold you up and hope for the best. So that's what I did. Ran and ran and ran. Must have been ten or fifteen minutes later before I hit bottom, where the ground leveled out and helped me slow down to a stop. I think I was a little hysterical, laughing like a madman."

Simon leans back again in his chair, staring at that candle. Then he reaches his hand out to pull the candle toward him, touching the soft wax dripping from under the flame. "Exhilaration," he says, sort of quiet. "That was my brother. Teaching me exhilaration."

"How did he die?" Tim asks.

Simon looks up from the candle at Tim and me. "Motorcycle accident," Simon says, and suddenly I'm surprised that I've never wondered more about him. Never really thought of him as anything but my teacher. Never imagined that he might be somebody's brother.

"He sounds cool," Tim tells Simon, and Simon sort of nods.

"He was."

As Tim heads out of the silent study room, I dangle my arm around Simon's shoulders while Stacy swings through the double doors on the opposite side of the glass wall. "It doesn't seem right when people die before they're old," I say.

Stacy's headed straight toward us. "Before they're supposed to." I lean against him, wishing his brother could come back somehow. Wishing I could tell him about Stacy's father. Simon loops his arm around my waist and squeezes. Stacy shoots in, stops short halfway to the desk, and sets her hands on her hips. Her hair is in a top-of-the-head ponytail today, splashing around her face like a waterfall.

"School is not supposed to be a lovefest, you know!"

I pull away from Simon and head for the front room. "Come on." I tug her out with me. "Let's go sit with Tim."

At recess Danny tells us we're going to scrimmage St. John's a few weeks after the camping trip. As sort of a pre–fall season practice.

"They're the best team in the league," I say, juggling the ball. "How did Simon get them to agree to play us? They don't even know who we are yet." Danny tries a steal, but I fake him out, and he ends up on his butt. Our dirt field has gotten softer in the past few weeks, slowing us down by just the littlest bit.

"I heard Simon talking to Maggie before lunch," Danny goes, brushing off his jeans. "They only said okay to a scrimmage because they know we have a girl on our team and they think they're going to cream us." I kick the ball backward over my head to Tim, who's behind me. He traps it. "They think that we'll be a waste of time next fall and that if they beat us now, we won't want to play in September."

"Well, St. John's is in for a surprise," Tim goes, and I feel a little hop of excitement at the idea of actually getting to play another team. A real team.

Later, right before messing up a corner kick, I see Stacy standing near the field, alone, watching us. I don't have a chance to wave or call out to her right then, and when I look up again, she's not there.

I think I imagined her until the afternoon, when I'm working on a book–movie comparison of *Little Women*, sitting next to Marie in the back room. Stacy glides in with two mythology books and plops herself next to me. I'm about to ask her if I can tell Tim about her dad, as long as I swear him to secrecy, but she beats me to talking.

"You're good," she says. I think she means at soccer.

"I thought I saw you watching," I go. She nods. "I figured you'd be at the ladder," I tell her.

"I was." She tips her chair back. "But I wanted to see what you were up to."

"What do you mean, up to?" I ask. "You make it sound like we're not really playing soccer or something."

She clumps her chair down and leans in, making her tongue ring click against her teeth. “Well, you’re not.”

“Huh?”

“Stacy thinks you ought to bring the boys down to the stream sometimes,” Marie explains, trying to squash a clay Sphinx’s nose so it looks broken off, like the real one in Egypt.

“What for?”

“We’ve got to have a chance at them too,” Stacy says. Then she lowers her voice. “You have to share.” She’s leaning so close now that her high ponytail is bobbing above my forehead.

“Yeah,” Marie goes. “You can’t have the boys all to yourself anymore.”

“You’re crazy,” I say to Stacy. Anybody can play soccer or be at the stream anytime. People go where they want. I don’t have anything to do with it.

“Well, you can’t,” Stacy says. Then she looks at Marie. “Except for Tim and Simon. Tim belongs to Alex, and Alex belongs to Simon.”

“What are you talking about?” I say. She’s making me and Tim sound all wrong. Like we’re boyfriend and girlfriend or something. And she’s making Simon and me sound like . . . I don’t know. Like something completely weird and gross. It’s making my face all hot.

"Simon's a *teacher*," Sophie goes, loud from the kitchen hallway, where she's collecting bacteria for Science Unit Seven. She's Maggie's daughter, and usually she stays pretty quiet. Maybe because if you're the principal's daughter, it's just better not to call a lot of attention to yourself.

"Come on," Stacy moans, like we're all dense or something. "It's natural for guys and girls to like each other."

"Are you serious?" I go.

"If you're not getting any work done," Simon calls, surprising us by poking his head out of the silent study room, "there's an empty table right here." I want to get out of here and take that table, but now I can't. Not after what Stacy's just said. So I sit still, watching Simon's candle flame flicker through the glass wall, feeling like a jerk.

"We're done," Stacy tells him, like we've settled some big question. "We'll be quiet now." She opens one of her books. I stare at my book–movie comparison while Simon stands at the door, watching us. By the time I hear him go back to his desk a few seconds later, my stomach is clamped tight.

I try to talk to my mom about it after dinner. She's lying on her side of the bed, thumbing through stacks of magazines.

I lie on my father's side of the bed, looking all of them over. They're mostly serious, with covers of politicians on trial for different crimes or war pictures from Africa or the Middle East. But there's a *Mad* magazine thrown in too, with Alfred E. Neuman grinning his wide, stupid grin. My father must have put that one there. I leave it alone, hoping it will make my mom smile, which will make my dad smile, which will balance out how upset they get over the other covers.

"That new girl is sort of confusing," I finally say, after there's no more magazines to stall over. "I mean, I like her, but she can be really obnoxious." My dad walks out of the bathroom in his pajamas and with a wet head. He snaps his towel to scoot me to the foot of their bed.

"Don't bounce," my mom says. She's staring at a magazine, but she's not reading it. You can tell because her eyes aren't even moving.

"Mom, did you hear me?" I say.

"You okay?" my father asks her, rubbing the towel over his orange hair.

She smiles her spacey smile at us. "Fine," she goes.

"She's such a bad liar, isn't she, Alex?" my dad says. He sinks onto the bed, with his back leaning against the headboard and his legs stretched out.

"Yeah," I go, wiggling farther down and pulling up my knees, to give him room.

"Okay," my mom says to us. "Here's a question." She

tosses the magazine onto the floor. “It’s an old question. One people have debated since the beginning of time.”

My dad squinches his toes against my knees. It’s sort of like a massage and a tickle at the same time.

“Stop,” I tell him. He stops. “What’s the question?” I ask my mom.

“If a man steals, should he always go to jail?”

“Yeah,” I say.

“Why?” my mom says.

“Because it’s against the law to steal.”

“But what if the thief has a good reason?” my mom asks.

“Like what?” I go.

“Like what if the man stole medicine that he was too poor to buy, but he needed it to save the life of his child?”

“Oh,” I say.

“See?” she goes.

“Well, couldn’t the man have asked for help or money or something?” I try.

“He asked already, several times, and nobody gave it,” my mom says.

“Oh,” I go.

“See?”

“So who is it’” I ask.

“The man?” she says.

"Yeah."

"Actually, it's a woman," my mom says. "And she didn't steal medicine, exactly. She stole an illegal drug she's addicted to. If she doesn't take it regularly, she gets really sick. So sick that she can't take proper care of her two kids."

"So why not help her get un-addicted and have someone else take care of her kids in the meantime?" I go. "Like, put them in foster care or something?"

"She's tried that a few times. Both times her kids were worse off than when they lived with her. Both times she got clean for a little while to get them back, but then she got addicted again."

"Well, maybe she's just a bad person, and she's just scamming everyone," I say. "Maybe she shouldn't have kids and she should be in jail."

"Is that really what you think?"

"I don't know," I go. "It's hard."

"It is, isn't it?" my mom goes.

"What do you think?" I ask.

"I know her," my mom says. "I've been treating her. She's complicated, and I like her, and I don't think she's a bad person. But I'm having some difficulty figuring out what is true about her and what isn't."

"How come you have to figure it out?" I go.

"Because, as her oncologist, I have to submit my professional opinion of how and where she should or can spend the rest of her life."

"Oh," I say.

"I want to be fair," my mom says. "It's so important to be fair."

"That sucks, Mom."

"Thanks," she says.

"What about you?" my dad asks me. "You were saying something about your new girl. She's acting out?" That's psychiatrist talk. It means you misbehave or have an attitude because you're feeling bad or weird about something.

"Maybe," I say. I pick up the *Mad* magazine and stare at the cover. Alfred E. Neuman has a tooth gap, just like Stacy's. "She said these gross things today."

"What kind of gross things?" he asks.

"Just stuff about people liking other people."

"Yeah, that sounds pretty disgusting," my dad says.

"You know what I mean," I say. "*Like* like. Not regular like. *Like*, as in 'romantically interested.'"

"Aren't you a little old to think romantic interest is gross?" my mom asks.

"It's just gross because of who she says likes who. She's got all the wrong people matched up." I sound completely idiotic. But all of a sudden, it seems too complicated to even explain.

"Maybe she's trying to get people's attention," my mom says.

"Well, she's got it," I go.

"She's probably nervous, being new and all," my dad tells me. "Give her a day or two to relax, to settle in a little," he says. "I bet she'll stop acting out before the week's even over."

6

I DECIDE THAT my father's right about the acting out and that Stacy just said that obnoxious stuff because she's still having messed-up feelings about her father dying and all, which make her not think so straight all the time. My dad thinks people act out less when they talk more about stuff. So maybe Stacy might spaz down if she'd just start talking about her big secret to Tim, or maybe even to Simon. And maybe she'd start talking about it if she had some hard-to-ignore reason to explain stuff. Some hard-to-ignore thing that Simon and Tim would ask her about, even though they both know what that thing means already. And something that might make her feel better at the same time.

So I dig around in our junk drawer through half-used

memo pads, a snowman paperweight, different sized batteries, a broken pair of sunglasses, safety scissors, masking tape, a metal whistle, and a deck of cards. What I'm looking for is a candle, and I find a small green one in the back corner. It smells like pine trees, and it's perfect.

I want to get Stacy alone after flash cards and before Tim's oral report. But it's hard because Stacy's mom drops her off late, and then Stacy totally ignores Simon's instructions to go outside and wait quietly by the downhill wall for Tim's demonstration. Instead, she sneaks into the back room to coach Teddy on three-card monte. It's this game where you have two red cards and one black one, and you switch the cards around as fast as you can, facedown. Whoever's playing you has to guess which card is the black one. You win if they can't guess, and they win if they guess right. Teddy's not that good at it yet, but he's getting better.

"Once you monte me," Stacy's telling him when I finally find her, "you could start betting money on the game." He's concentrating so hard, swapping those cards back and forth, he doesn't even answer her. "Okay?" Stacy goes.

"Mmkay." Teddy's pudgy hands are flying.

I grab Stacy's bony wrist. "Come on," I say. "I've got something for you." She looks tired. She has blue veins bumping up from the skin under her eyes, and her hair's sort of messy. No ponytail or anything.

"Really?" She follows me into the side kitchen hallway. "So." She crosses her arms. "What is it?"

I pull the candle out of my back pocket. "I don't know exactly when your dad died," I tell her, talking fast "But you light this when it's been a year. And then every year after that. To remember." Stacy takes the candle from me. She turns it over in her hands and then picks some wax off the wick with a stubby fingernail.

"Oh, man," she goes.

"It's supposed to help you feel better. Sort of." I brace myself, hoping she won't be mad at me for even bringing it up.

"You're nuts," she whispers. It's the first time I've ever heard her speak as soft as that. "Completely nuts." She tilts her face so that she can smell the evergreen, and her hair falls around her cheeks. I wait for a while, but Stacy seems like she's forgotten I'm there.

"We should go," I say, turning away from her. "Tim's probably about to start." When I push through the double doors onto the slate path, Stacy's right behind me, but when I look back at her, I don't see the candle anywhere.

Most of our class is already at the back wall at the foot

of the hill when Stacy and I get there. I push my sweater sleeves up on my arms because even with the breeze, it's almost warm out today.

"Shorter people up front," Maggie keeps saying. She's already biting her lower lip. Maggie came on one camping trip two years ago, and she hates this stuff. It makes her nervous. She's always muttering the words my parents were using the other night; words like *liability* and *accountability*. Sometimes *lawsuit*. Sophie's standing as far away from Maggie as possible. Right next to Viv.

"Are you ready down there?" Simon yells to us, from the roof.

"Ready!" we shout back.

We all get really quiet, waiting for Tim to appear over the edge of the roof. Then he does, easing out smooth, planting his feet flat on the wall, creeping downward.

"Cool," Danny says, and we all nod. Even though most of us have seen Simon rappel, and even though some of us have even done it with Simon on camping trips, it's still something to see.

"I'm going to do that one day," Sebastian tells us. "I swear I am."

"You shouldn't swear," Marie goes.

"Shut up," Danny says.

"You shouldn't say shut up either," Marie says.

"God," Stacy goes to them, and they shut up as Tim pushes out from the wall with his feet and then kind of bounces down. His backward hops seem to be going okay until he gets to the middle of one of the building's huge, round windows. That's when he starts moving quickly and has to pull on the rope to slow down. But the rope must be tangled or something, because Tim starts swinging from side to side, faster and faster, like an out-of-control pendulum on a giant grandfather clock.

"He's going to crash," Sebastian goes. "He's going to wipe out, big time." Stacy grabs my arm and bites hard on her hair.

"Pull up," we hear Simon say from the roof. But Tim can't. "Up, Tim. Pull up."

Don't fall, Tim, I think as hard as I can. *Don't fall.* He's whipping all around, with long yanks that snap his body back and forth, and for a split second I feel what it would be like if he died.

Stacy pats my shoulder. "He'll be all right," she whispers, and that makes me feel better, and then Tim gets control of the rope, yanks up hard, and slows way down. When he finally hangs straight and perfectly still, he lifts his arms and then pushes off with his feet and hops all the way to the ground. As soon as his toes touch grass, we go wild, cheering and whistling, and by the time Tim loosens the ropes around his thighs and takes off his helmet, Simon's there, clapping him on the back and shaking his hand. Then Tim starts.

"Rappelling is a way of going down a rope by using friction as control," he says, shuffling forward as best he can with all those ropes still dangling off him. "Friction is kind of hard to explain, but it has to do with the kind of motion between two things that are moving against each other, and it has to do with how fast they're moving and whether they're the same size and made of the same stuff. So the way two pieces of rope move against each other and slow each other down, or don't, is sort of an example of friction."

Simon moves backward into the crowd, like he always does during oral reports, to make sure you're speaking loud enough. I get ready to ask the question Tim's planted, concentrating on what he's saying so I won't miss my cue. But Stacy pokes me and leans in close.

"Friction," Stacy goes, like it's something dirty. "Get it?" I don't. She makes a circle with her thumb and index finger and then slides her other index finger in and out of it. Which is a way of showing sex, which I do get. And which Tim sort of notices. I can tell by the way his eyes go wide for a second and how he has to start the sentence over that he was in the middle of saying.

"Stacy!" I grab her hands to hide what she's doing. "Simon will see!"

"So?" she goes, but she stops.

"Usually people rappel down . . . Usually they go down mountains or off cliffs for sport or for rescuing skiers and rock climbers and stuff," Tim's saying. "But I just did it down the wall, since we're too far from Storm Mountain to have an oral report out there."

"Anyway," Stacy whispers, like she's just finishing a conversation we've already started, "Simon likes you." Oh no. Not this stuff again.

"Simon likes all of us," I hiss. Tim throws me a look, probably because I'm distracting him, but what am I supposed to do? Just let her say this stuff?

"No," Stacy goes, forgetting to whisper. "Simon *likes* you." Marie is totally staring at me and Stacy now, maybe because Tim keeps glancing at us. My stomach burns. Tim's trying to talk about all the different kinds of ropes you can use and what they're made of. But he's sort of rattled, and so am I, because Stacy's saying it straight out this time: that Simon *likes* me, in that boyfriend-girlfriend kind of way. And Marie isn't the only one who heard that. Teddy's neck is bright red, and Danny's grinning like a madman.

Simon's walking our way again, and Stacy leans on my foot with hers and presses her lips together at me in this knowing look.

"When you move the rope away from your body," Tim's saying. "Um, when you move it away, you . . . you get an unlocked position." He stops for a second and glances away from me and Stacy. "And you increase your speed. Then, um, . . . when you pull . . . when you pull the rope close to your body and behind your back, you get a locked position, and you can stop yourself." Now he glances back at us, just as Simon squeezes my shoulders as he passes.

"See?" Stacy goes, sliding her tongue ring back and forth over her upper lip. Gross.

"Simon's a *teacher*!" I tell her, even though I know she didn't care about that the last time she heard it.

"God." Stacy shakes her head.

Practically nobody's even looking at Tim now. They're all looking at me. Tim's still talking, but his voice is really high, and he keeps going, "Uh . . . uh," like he forgot what he had to say.

"Rappelling is, uh, an important part . . . Rappelling is an important part of my life because it's, uh, the best. It's the most, uh, fun thing I've ever done." Tim's totally glaring at me and Stacy.

Maggie starts to clap from somewhere in back of all of us. It takes a second for everybody else to join in, and when they do, it's lame. Simon steps forward to ask who has questions, but nobody does, not even me.

And Stacy's just standing there smirking.

7

I FIND TIM in the bathtub that sits at the back of the front classroom. It's one of those old-fashioned ones with lion paws holding it up and a fat lip all the way around that rises and curls like a small wave spilling up and over its own edge. The tub is filled with pillows. Tim's pretending to read in there, but he doesn't fool me.

"Let me in," I say. He doesn't move. I push his legs over myself to make room.

"You forgot to ask me about sleeping on the ropes," he says, throwing down his book.

I want to kill Stacy. "I'm sorry."

Tim won't even look at me. "Danny told me what she was saying."

"Yeah," I mutter.

"Why do you want to hang out with her, anyway?" he goes. But I don't want to. Not anymore. "She's a pain."

"Yeah," I say again. He looks surprised.

"I thought you'd be mad if I said that." His voice is really low.

"I'm not mad," I go. "She is a pain." The truth is the truth. She really is a royal pain.

Tim pulls a caribiner clip out of his pocket and snaps it in his hand over and over. The metal makes a sharp clicking sound. "She's such a pervert," he goes.

"I know," I go. "But her father died." There. I'm so pissed off, I don't even care about her secret anymore. Tim stops snapping his caribiner. "He was in a car accident, and they're this religion that doesn't allow blood transfusions, so he died."

"Nuh-uh." He sits up straight, pushing aside an orange pillow with little mirrors sewn all over it.

"She made me promise not to tell because she doesn't like people asking her stuff all the time."

"No way."

"Way." I nod. I'm glad I broke my promise. Glad I'm sharing secrets with Tim again. "You can't say a word," I whisper. "She'll slaughter me if she finds out I told."

"I know," Tim whispers back.

* * *

Something about Stacy bugs me enough that I'm still worrying a whole week later. So I find Simon in the silent study room. Everybody else is getting ready to go home, but I really need to talk to him.

We leave the day after tomorrow on our camping trip, and I'm nervous Stacy's going to do something. I don't know what, exactly. I just know I'm nervous.

"What's up?" Simon goes, as soon as I walk in.

"What do you think of Stacy?" I ask him. He's straightening up piles on his desk, throwing things away, stacking papers in different trays, shutting down his laptop.

"Anytime one person asks another what they think of a third, it's usually because the first person has a pretty strong opinion to begin with," Simon goes. I have to think a minute to sort out what he's saying, but then I get it

"I like her and I don't like her," I say. It's hard for me to look at him with everything Stacy's been saying, so instead, I look through the glass wall and watch all the kids gathering stuff from their lockers.

"Well, you've got a real situation, then, don't you?" Simon goes. He stops messing with his desk and sits up on the edge of it instead. "Okay. So tell me what you like about her."

"She's sort of cool. At least, she can be sort of cool."

"Now that's a descriptive word," Simon goes. "*Cool.* That says just about everything anybody would want to know."

"Come on, Simon." I shove his knee. "You know what I mean." I guess he can tell I'm not in the mood for a vocabulary lecture, because he lets it drop.

"All right," he says. "Fine. So what don't you like about her?"

"She's just . . . She says messed-up things. Really messed-up stuff."

"Uh-huh," Simon goes.

"I wish she wouldn't," I say. The bus kids are leaving now, pushing through the double doors onto the slate path. "I don't know. At first it seemed good to have another girl around. Someone who wasn't so, you know, girly."

"Stacy doesn't strike me as girly," Simon goes.

"She's not," I say. I guess that's part of what I like about her. Liked about her. I lean against the desk, and through the glass, I watch Tim look around in the front room. He spots me and waves for me to come out. Stacy turns around from her locker and starts waving at me too.

"Stick with her," Simon goes. "You two just need to wrestle things out." And he scoots over and pulls me into a roughhousing headlock. Three things happen right then that fill my gut with jackhammers: Simon's hand brushes my chest accidentally; Tim's wave freezes in the air; and Stacy plants her hands on her hips, raises her eyebrows, and mouths, *I told you so,* through the glass wall.

I pull away fast from Simon, but he doesn't seem to notice. He just pushes my head playfully toward the door and then turns to lift his bike off its hooks.

It's dark out, and I'm supposed to be in bed, but instead, I'm bobbing in my rocking chair, nervous. For one thing, I'm worried about what Tim and Stacy are thinking. Tim must know it was just an accident. It's Stacy who will try to make a big deal out of it. After it happened, I couldn't catch up to either one of them because Simon asked me to carry some recycling crates from the upper school to the lower school. So I have to figure out what to do if Stacy brings it up. I don't think trying to ignore her is going to work.

I tip the rocker back and forth, feeling my nightshirt sliding over my skin. And now my mind wanders to something else. Something I haven't been able to get out of my mind. Just this little thing: the way it felt when Simon's hand brushed my chest. Warm and soft where it touched, but then, just for half a second, a kind of melting and sliding everywhere else.

It's not like I have much. I don't even wear a bra yet, mostly because I don't need one. But something funny happened when he touched me there anyway. I wouldn't admit it to anybody because it's gross thinking that feeling came from my teacher. Still, the feeling itself was nice. I'd like to have it again. Just not with Simon.

"You look pooped," my father tells me at the breakfast table. He's pulling on his socks and shoes. My parents don't really eat breakfast. The kitchen is just where they finish up getting ready for work so they can keep me company while I eat. The rule is I have to eat something. They don't. Typical.

My mom comes down the back stairs, strapping on her watch and checking out my face at the same time.

"Are you okay?" she asks. She rests the back of her hand on my forehead.

"I guess I didn't sleep so good," I say. I've got a bowl of Rice Chex all poured with milk in front of me, but I'm not very hungry.

"Maybe you were too cold," my mom goes. "You don't feel sick, though."

"I wasn't too cold. I'm fine. I just . . . I was thinking a lot."

"What were you thinking about?" my mom asks. I want to try to explain what's been happening. But some of it's sort of personal, plus it's hard to describe, especially to your parents.

"It's that new girl, Stacy," I start anyway. "She's still being disgusting."

"What's she saying now?" my dad asks.

"She's sort of . . . It's like . . . Well, first of all, she acts kind of older than the rest of us. I mean, she is older, because she's fourteen, but—"

One of their beepers goes off. They both pat their pockets, and my mom pulls hers out and looks at it.

"Oh," she goes, biting her lip. She glances at my dad. "It's Martha."

"Alex, listen," my dad says. "That's the patient of mom's who's really, really sick, the one with the kids."

"The addicted one?" I go. "The thief?"

"She doesn't beep us unless something is very wrong. Like an emergency."

"We want to hear what's going on," my mom adds as she heads for the garage door. "We truly do, sweetie. So let's talk again tonight, okay?"

It's not like I have a choice. Some addict woman with little kids is dying and everything, and my problem is so small, I don't even know how to put it into words.

"Yeah," I say. "Okay."

* * *

We don't do flash cards in the morning because we're supposed to spend the whole day preparing for our camping trip. Tim, Stacy, Sophie, and I are organizing the rappelling equipment, which includes picking knots out of the ropes and then coiling each line, all neat and even and everything. I slide my hand from one end of a line to the other, so I can smooth it as straight as possible before I start to coil. Tim does the same thing, using his thumb and index finger as a loop. Stacy watches him and lifts her eyebrows up under her bangs, which are combed forward today.

"Friction," she goes.

"Yeah, right," I say.

"Here's more," Sophie tells us, and she puts a pile of tangled ropes on our table.

"I bet Simon loves friction." Stacy smirks, running her tongue ring across her lower lip.

"It was an accident," I go.

"What was an accident?" Sophie asks. Not nosy. Just curious.

"He felt her up," Stacy says.

"He did not!" Tim goes.

Walk away, I tell myself. *Walk away.* But I can't. "It was a mistake," I say to Sophie. She picks out one of the tangled clumps from the table and starts to work on it, all casual.

"I'll get this one," she goes, like she isn't even hearing this.

"Quit making stuff up, Stacy, or I'm not talking to you anymore," I say. "I swear."

Stacy snorts.

"I mean it!" I leave my ropes alone and stare her in the eye. She stares right back, and I will myself not to blink. Finally she looks down.

"Okaay," she groans, and I think I've won. But when almost all the lines are neatly coiled, Stacy starts up again.

"I just think it's kind of strange that a grown man wants to spend his weekend with a bunch of kids."

"We're not a bunch of kids," Tim goes. "We're his kids."

"We are not his kids," Stacy says. Tim stops working with his rope. I glance over at Sophie. She's staying quiet.

Stacy runs her hands up and down a line. It's nasty the way she's doing it. She's purposely making it nasty.

"You watch," she tells us. "How much you want to bet Simon ends up sleeping next to Alex?"

"He has his own tent!" I go.

"Oh, please," Stacy says, rolling her eyes. Sophie stands up and walks away.

"You are so full of it," Tim tells Stacy.

"You are," Stacy says.

"Why don't you ever try being human?" Tim goes.

"Forget it, Tim," I say.

"Why don't you kiss my ass?" Stacy goes right back at him. "Simon's a pervert, stupid!"

"Stop," I say.

"You're the pervert!" Tim tells her, pushing out his chair and jumping to his feet.

Stacy leans back, crossing her arms, all calm. "Screw you," she goes.

"Stop it!" I say again.

"Just shove it, Stacy!" Tim yells, and he grabs a rope and snaps it hard on the floor. It cracks, loud, and Stacy leans forward and slams her hands on the table.

"You shove it and die!" she yells back at him.

And the next thing I know, I'm standing on top of the table between them, shouting, "Stop it! Stop it!" over and over, and then Simon is there, and he yanks me down, and Tim and Stacy are so surprised at me that Tim drops the rope and their mouths stay closed tight all the way to the principal's office.

"I want that glass sparkling," Maggie orders us, handing over buckets, rags, and a step stool. She's talking about the round windows. They're high up off the ground and four feet in diameter. Four feet from any edge to any opposite edge.

Huge. Like big, round eyes, wide open, just begging you to daydream right through them. The windows aren't so great, though, when you have to wash them.

"By the time that glass is clean," Maggie's telling us, "I want to know the three of you can work together in peace."

I grab a bucket and stare at the carpet. Tim and I have never, ever gotten into trouble.

"This is illegal," Stacy complains. "Making us do the janitor's job."

"Would you rather I call your parents?" Maggie asks. *Parent,* I want to say. "Because I will if you feel you're being treated unfairly." Stacy glances at me and then grabs the other bucket.

"Whatever," she goes.

But when we're almost finished with the first window, she can't help herself.

"This is all your fault," she accuses me. She flicks her rag at Tim's leg. "Right, Tim?"

"My fault?" What is she talking about?

She begins to giggle. "Yeah, because you're such a troublemaker."

"Bull," I tell Stacy. "It's your fault." I look up at Tim, who's on top of the step stool. "Yours too," I tell him. And it's true. He didn't have to go ballistic like that.

"Me?" he goes. "But Simon is *not* a pervert!" He glares at Stacy. "Right?"

"God," Stacy moans out. What does that mean? I try to catch Tim's eye, but he's looking at her instead of at me.

"It's her fault," Stacy says again, nodding toward me and smirking. She really is full of it. But Tim cracks a grin.

"Huh," he goes, like he's thinking about it, and he hops down. I don't get it.

"Huh is right." Stacy nods.

Tim looks at me and shrugs. "Maybe." Which makes Stacy snort. I can't believe it. Stacy flicks her rag at Tim's leg again. He flicks her back.

"You guys better quit it, or Maggie's going to make us clean the whole school," I warn them.

"See?" Stacy goes. I don't see, but now Tim's sort of laughing too.

"Yep," Tim goes.

"Stop it!" I tell him.

"Sorry," he says, but when Stacy snorts again, he starts laughing for real.

"Tim!"

"Tim!" Stacy mocks me. And now they're doubled over. I whack both of them on the legs with my rag, pretending as hard as I can to think they're funny.

8

USUALLY I'M SO excited on the morning of our camping trip that I can hardly stand it. But everything starts off bad this time.

"See you," I go to my dad, hoping to get out the door before my mom gets downstairs and the two of them start grilling me.

"Wait," my father says, trying to help me hoist on my backpack, even though I didn't ask him to. "Aren't we driving you? This thing is really heavy."

"Nah," I say. "I want to walk."

The truth is, I don't want my parents to find out about the fight yesterday, and also, I don't want to cry in front of them. Which is what's going to happen if I have to talk about Stacy's bull and Tim messing with me the way he did, right along with her.

"We never really finished that conversation from yesterday morning," my dad says. "About your new girl. It seemed kind of important."

"Everything's okay," I lie. "Except I'm going to be late if you don't say good-bye already."

So he says good-bye and yells up to my mom, who runs down half dressed to tell me to have a good time, and now, feeling guilty and bad and all messed up in the head and sweating like crazy, I practically fall down the last stretch of wood trail onto Maple Avenue's shoulder. I have to stop and take my backpack off to adjust the straps and then get the thing back on again, and by that time I just want to scream.

"Tomy," Simon's saying as I walk into the upper school. *To cut,* I automatically think.

"Whose oral report today?" I ask Tim, sliding into the seat he's saved for me. It's the only seat left, or I might not have even taken it. I'm glad Stacy's not sitting next to him.

"Teddy's," he goes, passing his paper forward. Flash cards are over. "Where were you?" I shrug. "Stacy's doing it again," he whispers.

"Doing what?"

"Saying things about you and Simon."

"What things?"

"You know," Tim goes. "People are starting to believe

her." *That's what you get for egging her on,* I want to yell. But he looks so worried. Just like how I feel.

"What should I do?"

"I don't know."

I try to tell myself nobody's going to buy Stacy's stories over the truth. Still, I don't like it. I don't want people to think about Simon like that. Or about me like that either. It's too disgusting.

Teddy waddles in from the back hallway to the science counter in front of the room. He's guiding a shorter, rounder version of himself by the neck. For a second I forget about Stacy.

"This is Joey," Teddy tells the class. We're cracking up. "He's my little brother. He's nine years younger than me." Joey looks exactly like Teddy. Chins and all. He's glancing all around, kind of scared. I don't blame him. When I was in the lower school, I was kind of scared of the big kids. Now, I guess, my whole class is the big kids.

"How old are you, little Joe?" Teddy goes.

"Four," Joey says in this squeaky cartoon voice. Teddy smiles. He seems different up there today. Fatter or older or something.

"Joey's a fundamental part of my life because he's my little brother and brothers are ineffably important." Teddy lets go of Joey's neck and puts his arm on Joey's head. "He's my oral report." The whole class is going nuts. Stacy's laughing so hard over at her table, she's having trouble staying in her chair. She's wearing a headband. When she finally notices me, I glare at her, to let her know she better stop making things up. With all her clowning around, though, I'm not sure she gets it.

I look for Simon at the back of the room. He's not laughing at all. He has an expression on his face that's sort of twisted and familiar. It's the same one I saw that day with the candle, when he first told me and Tim about his brother, Andrew. It's this kind of confused, alone look. It crushes my stomach and makes me want to walk over and say something, anything, to Simon. Or just to sit next to him. Only now, because of Stacy, I can't.

We get in one quick game before it's time to load up the cars and leave for Storm Mountain. And things get more complicated on the soccer field.

"What's the deal with you and Simon?" Danny asks, tipping the ball to me for the kickoff. His hair's growing out, so you can see the black roots underneath the blue.

"There is no deal," I go, passing back to Tim and thinking that if I say it extra loud, nobody will hear my heart butting at my chest.

"Stacy says Simon made a pass at you," Danny says as Teddy tries to beat me to a throw-in. Teddy's fast, for a fat person, but I win the ball and kick it hard, right between his legs. Teddy doubles over and makes that *auugghh* sound guys make when they get clocked in the crotch.

"Dead babies!" Danny yells, and everybody runs over to Teddy. The game automatically stops when someone gets hit in the balls. That's because the hit person usually ends up curled in a sideways bundle on the ground, and the other boys get all tense and can't play for a few minutes. I watch Tim wince and cross his own legs. Viv gets on his knees and talks to Teddy.

"Try to breathe, man," Viv goes. "Just try to breathe it out." Viv is always so calm.

"You really nailed him," Tim tells me.

"It was an accident," I lie.

"So?" Danny asks me, quiet, while Teddy tries to sit up.

"So?" I go. "What?" But I know he still wants to hear about Simon.

"Is it true?"

"Don't be stupid," I say. "Stacy makes things up." Danny doesn't look so sure. "Anyway, Simon's a man," I say. "I'm just a girl."

Danny raises his eyebrows and looks right at my chest.

Then he leans in close to my ear. "Not for long," he whispers. And even though he hasn't touched me, I'm scared I'll get that soft melting feeling right here on the soccer field, and they'll all be able to tell. So I shove him. But before he can shove me back, these three workmen show up. They've got spades and rakes and a bunch of other tools, and when I glance down to the parking lot, I see two trucks.

"Sorry, kids," one of them says. "But you got to clear out of here."

"Oh," Viv goes. "I forgot."

"Forgot what?" Tim asks.

"My dad's donating sod for the soccer field. I guess before they put it down, they have to do stuff to get the field ready."

"What's sod?" Tim asks.

"It's grass that's already grown," Viv says. "It gets cut into these longs strips, and then you just roll it on the ground like a carpet."

"We don't need grass," Danny goes. "We need real goalposts and nets. Why doesn't your dad just buy us that stuff instead?"

"My father didn't buy the sod," Viv says, real even. "He got it for free from a friend. My mom wanted it for our backyard, but I asked if we could have it instead."

"We do so need grass," Teddy goes to Danny. "The ball moves different on a good grass field than on dirt. It's a totally new game then. And if we want to be halfway decent in the league next year, we better get the feel of it." Teddy turns to Viv. "It's cool of your father to give it to us."

"Yeah," Tim goes, and he flips the ball right onto Danny's jerk head. "Idget."

Most of the others are pulling away in Teddy's dad's SUV while Tim helps Sebastian into the backseat of Simon's car. Stacy holds the front passenger door open for me.

"Why don't you sit up front" She smirks, and I want to strangle her.

"You can," I say.

"No, thanks," she goes.

"Go ahead," I say. "I don't mind."

"No, really," Stacy goes, "*I* don't mind."

"Would one of you get in already?" Simon goes.

Stacy beats me to hopping into the back, between Sebastian and Tim, and I don't say anything to her for the whole ride. She tries to get me to, once. She leans forward from the backseat behind me and pats my head. "Your hair smells like a fruit salad."

I just pull my head away and turn up the radio.

* * *

We get to Storm Mountain right before dark. It's a new camping spot we've never tried, about halfway to the top of the highest peak. Thick trees cover the whole mountain in all shades of green and brown, and the shining spaces of small creeks sparkle above and below us. Vines dripping with bunches of purple flowers are strung all over the trees and make a perfume smell in unexpected places, like stray patches of warm water in a cool lake.

"Let's put the mansion up here," I say to Tim and Sebastian. We're standing on a lopsided square of level ground.

Some of the parents, like Marie's, don't like girls and boys sharing the same tent. But most of them don't think it's a big deal as long as Simon doesn't care, and he doesn't. So a bunch of us always sleep in Sebastian's tent, which got nicknamed "the mansion" last year because it sleeps four adult-size people, easy, plus a kid can stand up in it. But it's kind of old and hard to set up. Last year it took Simon almost an hour.

Now Teddy's dad is lifting it out of Simon's car. "You kids need help with this?"

Simon shows up right as we're pounding in the last stake and brushing out the inside. He's got a big shovel and a grin. He claps his hands twice to get everybody's attention.

"Latrine information!" he calls.

"La-what?" Stacy goes.

"Toilets," Sophie tells her.

"See those trees there in the middle of that clearing?" Simon asks. "With all the daffodils about to bloom underneath?" I look to where he's pointing. There's a small clearing about a half a soccer field away from us that's got three tall evergreens in a tight triangle and sprinkles of yellow buds all around. "In there," Simon says, "are two pits."

"Pits!" Stacy moans. "We have to go in pits?"

"Bring leaves with you." Simon laughs. "And make sure they're not poison ivy."

"He's kidding, right?" Stacy asks. Then she pushes me with her shoulder. "I bet Simon's going to—," she starts, and I interrupt her fast.

"Let's help with the fire," I say to Tim. "I'm starved."

It takes a while, but as soon as the flames get going, we throw our tinfoil-wrapped potatoes and chopped vegetables into a portion of the fire Simon sectioned off just for cooking. And not too much later Simon puts me in charge of the marshmallows. I pass them out, making sure nobody gets any more than anyone else, and Marie shows Stacy all the different toasting techniques.

"You never did this in Girl Scouts or anything?" Marie asks Stacy.

"I wouldn't be caught dead in the Girl Scouts," Stacy goes. "But that's just me." Then she offers Marie her stick, which is the best one because it's really long, and pointed at one end.

I always set my marshmallows on fire. Then I wave them in the air to put out the flame, and when I have little popping bubbles and a black skin on a swollen lump, it's cooked just perfect. The taste of ash combined with sugar is the best, even when Simon warns me its carcinogenic that way.

"Carcino-what?" Danny goes.

"Causes cancer," Teddy says.

Tim toasts his marshmallows to a golden brown. He stands over the fire, rotating his stick as steady and patient as Simon pulls out splinters.

"I like the sparks," I tell Tim, waiting with him by the fading flames as he finishes his last one.

"Yeah," he says, looking up at the night. "They kind of look like that, don't they?" I look up too. Silvery stars are sprinkled all over the wide sky, like mica chips on a new blacktop. They're whiter than the orange sparks that crackle and snap into nothingness right in front of us, but still, I know what Tim means.

"Uh-huh," I go. "And if you stare at one for too long, it disappears."

9

STACY COMES BACK from the toilet pits and sees Sebastian stretched out right in front of the mansion's entrance flap. I was hoping she'd want to sleep in someone else's tent, but Sebastian asked her to help put up the mansion, which she did, flashing her tongue ring at me once, and all the other tents are spoken for.

"Swap with me," she orders Sebastian now. Her sleeping bag is balled up at the edge of the tent, next to Sophie's.

"I'm already in," Sebastian goes.

"Don't be a pain. Swap places."

"You're being the pain," Sebastian goes. Tim kicks me, soft. In the dimness of all our flashlights he rolls his eyes. I kick him back and roll mine too.

"Sleep over here," Sophie goes.

"I can't," Stacy goes. "I have to be by the door."

"It's a tent," Sebastian goes. "There isn't any door."

"The entrance, then," Stacy says. "Whatever. I have to face it. Come on. Get up."

"Spaz down," Sebastian tells her. "I'm not moving."

Stacy starts pushing at Sebastian. "I have to face the entrance!" She sounds serious. Her voice is all high pitched. Squeaky almost. "Sebastian!" She's sort of screaming. "Move!"

"Why do you have to face the entrance?" Sophie asks.

"Because!" Stacy's hair is all messed up and in her face.

"Move, Sebastian," Sophie says, sort of quiet. She reminds me of Viv sometimes, how she's always so mellow. *Reasonable,* my mother would say.

"Yeah," Tim goes. "Just move." So Sebastian does. It takes a while. Stacy waits, quiet, not looking at anyone. When Sebastian's finally out of the way, Stacy takes a long time setting herself up. She puts her feet right at the entrance and slides her flashlight inside her sleeping bag. Maybe she's afraid of bears or something. Not that where you sleep would matter in the end anyway, if a bear broke in.

"Maniac," Sebastian mumbles. But he doesn't really sound that mad.

"Shut up." Stacy's voice is back to normal.

"I'm challenged." Sebastian fakes sounding all hurt. "You're not allowed to tell me to shut up."

"Shut up," Stacy says again, but then I hear her giggle. "Cripple."

"Wench," Sebastian goes, and then both of them start cracking up.

On the short hike to the top of this year's rappelling cliff, I make sure to fall into step with Stacy. Our legs are exactly the same length, and so our steps are in exactly the same rhythm. I slow us down and make sure everyone else gets a little ahead of us. Then I take a deep breath.

"I have to talk to you." Stacy's hair is rolled into a shiny topknot today, with pieces falling around her ears. I watched her arrange it this morning. Her hands and fingers had moved quick, like a spider's legs dancing on its web.

"Okay." She drops her arm around my shoulder. "So talk."

"You've got to stop saying stuff about Simon and me."

"What stuff?" Her arm goes stiff. I lift it off me. Then I face her full on.

"Stace," I say.

"Al," she says back, flashing her tongue ring.

"Please stop spreading rumors."

"I just tell people what I see."

"No, you don't." I start walking again. "You lie." Stacy steps toward me and tosses her arm over my shoulders again. She does it so it would look friendly to anybody watching. But she pulls me extra close and grabs a fistful of my hair, and she's pulling hard. It hurts.

"Ow!" I yell. She claps her other hand over my mouth. That hurts too.

"I like you, Alex," she whispers, turning her fist slow, pulling tighter without having to yank. It burns my scalp, and tears spring right through my eyes. "But don't you ever call me a liar again." She lets go and jogs toward the head of our group. If I weren't so surprised, I wouldn't have let her get away. I would have punched her and stomped on her head. I wouldn't care what my parents or Simon or anybody would say. I wouldn't care if my stomach cramped forever. She better watch her back.

After Teddy's dad's group double-checks the ropes for frayed places and Simon's group double-checks his anchor knots, Simon heads off to the landing spot below us.

"All right, Alex," he says. "You're up."

"You go," I tell Tim, even though we all drew sticks to decide the order, and I drew the longest one.

"Why?" Tim goes. My scalp is still burning.

"Hurry up," Sebastian says. "We don't have all day."

"I don't want to be alone with Simon down there," I whisper to Tim. I'm about to add it's because of what Stacy will make up about it later, not because Simon would ever do anything to me, but I can't because everybody's getting impatient.

"Come on," Sebastian says again.

"Let's go, Alex," Teddy's dad calls.

"Tim's going first," I say. Tim opens his mouth, like he's going to say something, but then he closes it again, scrunching his eyebrows at me. *Please, Tim,* I think. *Just do it.*

His ride down is as smooth and straight as soda through a straw. The rest of us watch from above by lying down on our stomachs with our heads poking out over the edge, which gives you a real rush. Except my chest feels kind of sore leaning against the ground. At first I think I've bruised it or something, but then, as Teddy's dad is helping me get harnessed in, I think it's maybe because I'm finally growing something there.

"Ready?" Teddy's dad asks me. *For what, exactly?* I feel like asking.

"Ready." I ease backward, using my feet to find the side of the cliff. If I look down, I might panic, so I focus back and forth on my shoes and on what's out to my side. All those mountains and green-and-brown fields, dotted with yellow-and-blue clusters of wildflowers and traces of ribbony roads. You can't concentrate too much on how everything looks like a fairy tale because if you lose focus, you might get hurt. So, instead, I think about the beat of my body and feet: *Slap, pull up, pause, push out, slide down. Slap, pull up, pause, push out, slide dawn. Slap, pull up, pause, push out.* And at the last *slide down*, the ground rises up solid under me, and Simon and Tim smile big smiles and say I did great and pull me out of the harness and ropes, and I can't believe it's already over until my turn next year.

"Number three on her way!" Teddy's dad yells down as Stacy's bottom and legs appear from high above and then bounce toward us in clumsy spurts and stops.

Her ride is a little choppy, but she's not screaming or anything, the way Marie did a few years ago. When she's about two thirds of the way down, Stacy freezes. She's close enough now that we can see her face pretty well, and it's white.

"Stacy?" Simon goes. She doesn't answer. "Stacy, what's the problem?"

"I'm stuck!" Her voice has that tinny sound it gets when she's upset for real and not just for show. It's confusing to think that the person up there, scared, is the same one who tore my hair so hard earlier.

"It's okay, Stacy," Simon calls up to her. "You're over halfway."

"But I'm stuck!" she yells back, and a part of me wishes she really were.

"You are not stuck," Simon goes. "You just need a rest."

"Yes, I am, Simon! I'm stuck! I'm stuck!" She's yelling at the top of her lungs now, and from far above, I can see small faces poking over the top of the cliff like dolls' heads.

"Now listen up," Simon calls. He motions to Tim and me to come over and grab the rope. We do it, and he steps away, I guess so he can look up and talk to her easier. "Take a deep breath through your nose," Simon tells her calmly. "Okay? A deep breath through your nose. Then let it out slow through your mouth, slow."

"Slowly," Tim mutters, and I glare at him, but he doesn't even notice he's said it. Stacy starts kicking her feet, and the rope bucks in our hands. It's burning my palm, but I hold on.

"You breathe!" she screams, kicking her legs harder. "I can't!"

"Yes, you can. Now do it." She's quiet a minute, and I guess she breathes, because the rope stops twisting.

"Keep breathing," Simon goes.

"I am," Stacy snaps. We wait, staring up at her, like she's some kite caught in a telephone wire or a cat up a tree.

"Okay, now push your lower hand out. Just a little," Simon tells her. "The hand behind your back. Push it out." She pushes it out, and her body creeps downward. "Good," Simon calls. "Keep your eyes on your feet. Keep going just like that. A little at a time." Stacy creeps lower and lower, and pretty soon Tim and I loosen our grip and step away. She's so close, I can see a small rip in her left jean pocket.

"I hate this," Stacy's saying. "I'm not ever doing this again. I—"

And then there's a cracking sound, and suddenly Stacy's lying on the ground, and the rope is flying down from above, from the place where she was stuck. It winds through the air, hypnotizing me with its arc, until the torn edge slashes my face, and then Simon's bending over Stacy, and my cheek is stinging, like it's been cut with a knife.

"Don't move," Simon tells Stacy. She's trying to sit up. "Don't move." He runs his hands up and down her arms and legs.

"Don't touch me!" She pushes his hands away and jumps to her feet. Then she turns to Tim and me. She's grinning. "That last part was a blast!"

We can barely keep up with Simon. He's running on the trail to the top of the cliff. The sting in my cheek has faded a little underneath Simon's emergency-kit cream, and Stacy has a huge tear in the knee of her jeans, with a smear of blood showing through, but otherwise, everybody's okay.

"It looks like you got stabbed," Tim says, checking out my cheek.

"Tell everybody you won a fight," Stacy says. I ignore her.

"The rope broke," I say to Tim. I speed up a little because Simon's pulling ahead. "We checked it a bunch of times, but it broke anyway."

"It must have been a lump," Tim says. "Teddy's dad missed a lump."

"Is that what I got stuck on?" Stacy asks. Probably. And I thought she was just scared. We're almost to the top of the cliff, and Simon's still running. When we finally break off the path to the launch spot, the other kids and Teddy's dad are standing as still as store mannequins. It seems like they're not even breathing.

"Thank God," Teddy's dad goes when he sees Stacy jogging toward him.

Simon pounds right up to Teddy's dad, as close as Stacy usually stands to people.

"That fall could have been from the top!" Simon goes. Teddy's dad backs up a few steps.

"I know it," he goes. "Believe me. The rope must have—"

"Rope must have nothing. That was supposed to be triple-checked, Paul! Triple-checked!"

"Simon, the kids . . . ," Teddy's dad says. His voice cracks halfway through *kids*. I thought only boys' voices cracked like that. "Can we discuss this later?"

"Dad?" Teddy goes, and I wish he could fall right down a hole so he wouldn't have to see this. His dad puts his hand up, like he wants to pat Simon or something, but Simon jerks back just the way Stacy jerked away from him a few minutes ago. He spits on the ground and then runs his hands through his hair.

"I'm taking a hike," he says after a second. "Anybody who wants to come is welcome. Everybody else go back to the campsite with Paul."

I go with Simon. Mostly because I don't want to go back to camp so early in the day, watching Teddy's dad with that awful look on his face, like some sort of broken clown. And I know Sebastian will be moaning all afternoon about how he got gypped out of his turn down the cliff, and I'm not in the mood to hear that. Even though I don't know how to act with Stacy anymore, now that she did what she did this morning, I'm also still afraid to be wherever she's not because I'm worried about what she might say. She follows Simon first, after Tim, so it seems like the thing to do.

"Where are we going?" Danny asks. We're veering off the marked trail into more prickly underbrush. Simon doesn't answer. He just makes his humming noise.

"Hey, Simon," Stacy goes. "Danny asked where we're going."

"Sshh," Tim tells her.

"You sshh," she tells him back.

We follow Simon single file, making our way upward the whole time. My back is bent forward somehow, and my calves start to ache, but I'm not about to ask for a rest. Anyway, it doesn't look like Simon's going to stop for anyone.

We push our way up the mountain. It seems like forever, but maybe it's only an hour or something. We don't stop once, and my heart's beating like I'm running a marathon, and even though it's not hot out, I'm sweating everywhere—on my scalp and the soles of my feet and everything.

But then I'm so tired, and I'm concentrating so hard on not getting branches in my eye or my cut cheek, that my brain sort of fades into a kind of nowhere land. The next thing I know, I'm stopped and sitting in a flat space with miles and miles of the world on all sides. It takes me a minute to realize that Simon's hiked us up to the peak of the mountain.

He stops his humming—he probably stopped it a while

ago—and his smile is so wide, you couldn't fit it inside the mansion.

"Nice, huh?" he says. We grunt a little, which is the best we can do, we're so wiped. Simon throws himself on the ground in a front fall, catching himself on his hands so it looks like he's ending in a push-up, and then he just settles right on the ground, all stretched out on his belly.

Tim flops on his butt right next to four purple crocuses, takes a swig from his canteen, and then dumps the rest of the water all over his head. Stacy's lying flat, arms and legs wide, staring up at the sky. Viv and Sophie are leaning against each other's backs, drinking and drinking from their water bottles; and Danny's perched as close to the mountain's edge as he can get, looking like some sort of blue-and-black-headed alien animal.

I rest my head on Tim's legs, watching the sky turn into millions of white and black and orange dots, like when you rub your eyes hard and you make spots on the insides of your lids, and then, I guess, I'm asleep.

"Storm's coming," I hear Simon say from somewhere behind the darkness, and when I open my eyes, the air is bluish, with long shadows slinking out from the trees and from Sophie and Viv, who are standing up and stretching.

"What time is it?" Stacy asks.

"No time in the country," Tim and Simon answer together. I sit up, feeling pieces of dirt and grass fall from my hair and shoulders. My cheek still hurts, but not as bad as before. Stacy's shaking out her moppy topknot.

"Were we all sleeping?" I ask.

Simon nods. "Like babies," he says. Then he starts to jog away. "Ready?"

"For what?" Danny yells. "Jeez. Where are you going?"

"Better hurry up," Simon yells back, and he's gone.

Tim's the first one to get it. He grabs my arm and runs. "Come on!"

We're running down the mountain. We're flying down the mountain. Simon's not waiting, and he's not taking any trail, and that means if we stumble or fall, we'll be lost and that's it. My legs are racing, rolling, and I feel like a deer—graceful and certain—and the tilted Earth is like a magnet, pulling and pulling me down, and I change from a deer to a marble on a slide, moving faster and faster, and I couldn't stop even if I wanted to, and I can't see Simon at all, and I can barely see Tim, and I think the closest person behind me is Danny, but I can hardly even hear him. What I hear are my feet pounding on the ground, and the blood pounding in my ears, and the trees whipping past, and the only other sound is someone laughing, and that someone is me.

And it goes like that, on and on and on, until finally I see Tim running on flat grass, running and then slowing and falling in a heap next to Simon. And then I'm out of the woods, off the mountain's side, slowing and slowing and slowing, until my legs don't know what to expect, and they quit, pulling me into another heap next to Simon and Tim. Then the others burst out of the trees, and they stumble and fall and roll, like tumbleweed whirling in a ghost town, and they're laughing and laughing. And then Simon leans over to me and Tim, after we've all caught our breath, and says, "Do you remember Andrew?" We do, and I know Simon's passed on what Andrew gave him a long time ago. Feeling alive. Exhilaration.

10

THE FIRE'S ALREADY blazing when we get back to the campsite. I'm so hungry, just the cooling air makes my mouth water.

"Took you long enough," Sebastian goes when we show up, one by one, to poke at the tinfoiled hamburgers baking in hot ash.

"Yeah," Marie says. "Where were you guys?" It's getting gustier by the second, and the flames jump and cough with the wind. Marie's bundled in this green parka with fur around the collar. She's all zipped tight around the chin. She looks really warm.

"We hiked to the top," Viv tells her. His brown skin glows the color of tree sap now, near the fire.

"Then we had to book down because there's a hurricane coming," Danny says.

"Not a hurricane, stupid," Sebastian tells him. "There's no hurricanes around here."

Danny shrugs. "Whatever, man."

"Is Simon still mad?" Teddy asks. His face is bubblegum pink, from the wind and leftover embarrassment, I guess.

"He forgot all about it," I say. "Really." Tim nods and passes a poking stick over so Teddy can have a turn at flipping our dinner. Teddy tucks it under his arm and then holds his palms out to the sky. The air feels full somehow. Everybody's hair is curling.

"It's definitely going to precipitate," Teddy tells us.

"Better not rain until we eat," Stacy goes, and I could swear Mother Nature listens to her because it doesn't start to thunder or really pour until we've finished our whole meal, including two bags' worth of marshmallows.

It gets pretty cold in the mountains at night. I wear my long johns plus a sweatshirt plus my blue sweater, and I borrow Tim's poncho and Sophie's umbrella to get to the toilet pits. I've waited too long, and I have to go so bad, I could practically wet my pants. My flashlight cuts a bright path through the night, the steady beam spreading into the black distance. Swollen drops slip into the beam from nowhere, making grass blades bow and sparkle, reminding me of Simon's candle flame.

By the time I get to the three pines, I'm soaking and shivering, and the bundle of toilet paper I've been trying to keep dry in Tim's coat pocket is nothing but mush. Great. I veer away from the pits and shine my light toward a patch of brush where I know I can grab a handful of leaves, and that's when I see Simon. I see everything. His heavy arc of pee, his rain-slicked wet *thing* above a jiggling sack of skin, and a nest of brown hair. Everything.

He jumps about a mile high. His thing flaps up and then down, still spilling from its tip. I drop my flashlight.

"Whoa," Simon goes, and then he goes, "Jesus," and then, "Alex, is that you?"

I want to die of embarrassment right there and then.

"Sorry," I tell him, feeling around on the ground for my flashlight. A flicker skips into my eyes from the sky, and I automatically start counting to see how close the lightning is. Simon taught us that: Every second between lightning and thunder equals one fifth of a mile. *One, two . . .*

"Jesus," Simon says again. The mud and grass under my fingers are freezing, and my bladder's about to burst. *Three.*

Lightning fills the air just at the same time as another thunderclap shakes the ground. I see Simon kneeling right next to me, my flashlight in his hand. In the next second it's dark again, except for the skinny yellow path of the flashlight beam.

"Sorry," I say again. I stand up fast. "I should have made some noise or something." My face is so hot, I'm sure it must be sizzling the raindrops into puffs of steam.

"Not your fault," Simon goes. He steps backward. "Could have made a noise myself. Singing." He's trying to make it better, but there's no way. On top of everything else, the last thing I want to do is imagine him singing with his pants down. He hands me the flashlight. I keep it aimed at the ground. I guess neither of us wants to look at the other.

"I really have to go," I tell him. A water bead wiggles at the end of my chin.

"Oh," he says. "Sorry."

"Do you have any extra toilet paper?" I go. "Mine's ruined." He reaches under his raincoat and hands me a roll. Our fingers touch, wet and soft, and I jerk back fast.

"Alex, it's all right," Simon says. "Nothing you need to worry about." That makes me feel a little better. But still. "See you tomorrow?" Simon goes, like he wants to make sure I'm okay. So I try to sound okay.

"See you tomorrow," I say, and he steps away.

I'm shaking pretty bad, and I pee a little on my shoe, but I'm trying so hard to get Simon's thing out of my head, I barely even notice.

On my way back to the tent I try taking deep breaths to calm down. In through my nose and out through my mouth. I've never seen a man's thing before, besides my father's when I was really little, in the bathroom and stuff, which I can hardly remember. And I used to sometimes catch a glimpse of Tim's when we would change into swimsuits or during a sleepover. But that was back when we were too young for it to matter. I've seen pictures before. And I barely even remember that, either. I definitely didn't know men's things were so floppy and thick-looking and *sluggy*.

Lightning slices through the sky again, and I count. *One.* And then the thunder bursts right on top of me, piggy-backed by more light filling the air, and I see our whole campsite, clear as day. Two of the tents have been blown flat, with their flaps slapping on the ground. Simon and Teddy's dad are struggling over another. At the same time three shadows are pulling closed Simon's car door, and four more are running toward the van. And then, just as quick, it all disappears.

"You're soaked," Sebastian says when I slither inside the

mansion. All their flashlights are still on. Tim tosses me a towel. I'm so cold, it's hard to wrap my fingers around the terry cloth.

"Don't drip on me," Stacy orders. Screw her.

"Me either," Sebastian goes. All I want to do is get into my sleeping bag.

"Are you okay?" Tim asks as I crawl to my place next to him.

I think I'm going to say, *The storm's blown everyone's tent down.* Instead, I whisper, "I just saw Simon peeing!"

I regret it immediately.

"No way," Tim goes.

"Really?" That's Sophie. I didn't mean for anyone else to hear.

"Did you see his dick?" Stacy asks. I knew it. "Come on, Alex," she goes. "Did you?"

If I don't say something, she'll start in with her lies anyway. "Sort of," I say. I wiggle into my sleeping bag and then cross my arms and tuck my hands under my armpits to warm up.

"Oh, man." Sebastian's shaking his head. "Man."

"Was it hard?" Stacy goes.

"Gross!" I tell her, wondering why it would be hard.

"Was it?"

"Dicks only get hard for sex," Tim mutters. I didn't know that. Anyway, it doesn't matter.

"He was *peeing*," I say again. I should have kept my mouth shut.

"Did you see pee?" Stacy goes.

"Yes!"

"Still," she says, "how do you know he didn't *want* you to see his dick?"

If I weren't so freaking cold, I'd smack her. "You're sick, Stacy," I go. "You're totally disgusting."

"I'm not the one who checked out his *thing*," she goes.

"I did not check it out!" I yell. "It was just there!"

"And I'm not the one always staring at Alex like that either," she says to the whole tent, in her know-it-all voice.

"Like what?" Sophie asks.

"God," Stacy goes.

"Like a lech," Sebastian tells Sophie. "Right, Stace?"

"Great, Stacy," Tim goes. "Now you've got Sebastian full of this crap too." She groans and rolls her eyes again, and Tim snaps off his light, and then so do I. Stacy turns her light off and shuts up, for a change.

It takes me a while to fall asleep, partly because I'm so cold, but mostly because of everything else. My cheek is stinging again. The lightning's stopped, and the last count was seven seconds, so I know the storm's mostly passed. But the rain making fast thumps on the mansion's roof sounds like some kind of warning to me. Like millions of tiny people jumping up and down, screaming, *Watch out, watch out, watch out!*

I must have drifted off after all, because a noise is pulling at me. Someone's unzipping the tent from the outside. I pop on the flashlight fast, under cover of my sleeping bag, and get just enough brightness to see it's Simon crawling in. Stacy's sitting straight up, staring at him and breathing like she's just run down that mountain again.

"Whoa," Simon freezes in his crouch. "Stacy, it's okay. It's just me." Stacy's eyes are wide, and her chest is rising and falling for air. "It's just me," Simon says again. "Didn't mean to scare you." She breathes a little slower but stays stiff, upright. "Paul's tent is busted, and the cars are all spoken for," Simon whispers. "Thought I could keep dry in here with you guys." Still, he doesn't move until Stacy does. She slides over Sebastian, waking him up as she flips around him, so now she's between Sebastian and the tent wall.

"Hey," Sebastian mumbles, "I thought you had to be by the door."

"This is a tent," Stacy whispers back. "There isn't any

door." Simon turns on his light and crawls around everybody's feet. Nobody's asleep anymore. It's crowded now, with him in here, and we all have to cram tight to make extra room. Simon finally wedges himself between my wall and me.

"Told you," Stacy says. Sebastian sucks in his breath, and Tim stops squinting and rubbing his eyes. Everybody's really quiet. Not asleep quiet in a peaceful way, but awake quiet, in a way that you just know something's wrong.

"What's up?" Simon asks all of us, sitting into a cramped position with his arms wrapped around his shins and his chin on his knees.

"Ask her," Tim goes, meaning Stacy. He's daring her to say what she thinks to Simon's face.

"Don't look at me," she goes. Simon looks at me, instead. I have no idea what to say.

I wake up one more time. The quick, wet thumps on the tent have stopped, and the air feels thinner, clearer. My left arm prickles. I try to lift it, but I can't because Simon's arm is weighing it down. His leg is squished against my back too. He's fallen over onto his side. I squirm into a tiny sliver of space in the other direction as fast as I can, but not before I hear a flashlight's click and see Stacy sitting up and staring. I know what she's thinking.

"He's *asleep*!" I whisper to her. She shakes her head slow, like she thinks I'm an idiot.

The night doesn't go too well after that. I have a lot of bad dreams. In one I'm trapped in a school full of nothing but walls and hallways but no exits. I'm trying to help a little kid get out, but I don't know the way myself. Then suddenly the little kid turns into a monster with Simon's face, and then the dream turns into a movie, and I'm in the audience. Then I don't remember what happens, except when I wake up, it seems like the dream lasted all night long.

11

IN THE MORNING Simon's gone and so is everybody else. The window flaps of our tent are rolled down, and the sun makes a screen of shadows through the webbed netting. I touch the rough scab on my cheek, from just under my eye to my mouth. I'll tell my parents a branch scratched me, because they won't like the truth.

I'm shrugging myself out of my sleeping bag when Sebastian falls halfway through the entrance.

"She's alive!" he yells, and I drag him inside.

"Why didn't anybody wake me up?" I'm wondering what I missed. Stacy pokes her head in and crawls through.

"We went on a hike," she tells me, like nothing's happened. "After we found all the tent stuff. Everything got blown all over the place." She pretends she doesn't even notice me glaring at her. She's holding a bunch of toothpicks in her hand. Tim crawls in, and Sophie's right behind him.

"Tim tried to get you up," Sophie goes. "You wouldn't open your eyes."

"Simon told us to let you sleep," Tim says. I brace myself, waiting for Stacy to tell everyone what she thought she saw last night. But she keeps quiet. Viv crawls in next, with Teddy right after, and everybody scoots around on their butts to make room. Stacy holds out a handful of toothpicks. "Pick one," she tells me.

"Whatever it is," I go, "I'm not playing."

"Come on, Alex," Stacy goes. "It's spin the bottle." She holds up an empty water bottle. "Whoever gets the purple mark goes first." She holds the toothpicks out to me again. I look to Tim, but he just shrugs, kind of nervous.

"I'm not playing anything with you," I tell Stacy.

"God, Alex," she goes. "Why are you so afraid of a little game?" That's not what makes me change my mind. It's knowing that if I go outside and they hear Simon talking to me, there's no telling what she might say. So I pick a stupid toothpick. It looks regular to me. Viv goes next, and he gets the one with the purple ink at the bottom.

"That sucks," Sebastian goes. "I wanted to go first."

"Okay. Get in a circle," Stacy commands. We sit

cross-legged. Stacy arranges us: boy, girl, boy, girl. Teddy puts the bottle in the middle of our ring. We have to clear away some of the sleeping bags and mess kits to make room for the bottle to spin. I've never kissed anyone before, besides my parents, and that doesn't count, anyway. I'm not sure if this game is mouth kissing or cheek kissing or what, but I'm scared if I ask, Stacy will say something I don't want to hear.

Viv spins, and I hold my breath, hoping it doesn't land on me. It doesn't. It lands on Sophie. She looks down at her crossed legs but doesn't move a muscle. Viv gets up on his knees, I guess so he can lean over better. Teddy and Sebastian start to giggle, but Viv's not doing anything.

"For every second you wait," Stacy goes, "you have to keep the kiss going for two more seconds." When Viv still doesn't do anything, she starts counting. "One Mississipp—," she goes. Viv leans over really quick and kisses Sophie right on the mouth. So it's mouth kissing.

Sophie smiles a quick, small smile, and Viv sits regular again, pretending nothing much happened.

"Your turn," Sebastian says to Sophie. She spins the bottle, and it lands on Teddy.

"No tongue, please," he goes. "I don't like that French stuff." Sophie gives him a fish peck on the mouth. Teddy's neck turns pink. Big surprise.

"Come on," Stacy tells him. "Spin." He spins, but right at the same time Simon's face in one of the tent windows makes us jump.

"Let's go," he says through the netting. "We've got to be on the road soon. Your tent should be down already."

"I knew it," Sebastian goes when we hear Simon's feet scrunching away. "I never get my turn."

Viv and Sophie slip out of the tent together, and Teddy helps slide Sebastian out after them. Tim gets ready to go after Teddy, but Stacy blocks his way.

"Wait a minute," she says. "You guys never got a chance to kiss." My stomach does a little flip.

"That's okay," Tim says, glancing at me through his curls. He needs a haircut. I want to ask him why it's okay, because suddenly, even though I don't really want to either, it matters.

Stacy puts her hands on her hips. "It's not going to kill you, you know."

"They're waiting for us," I go.

Stacy rolls her eyes. "I thought you two were friends."

"We are," we both say.

"Friends kiss all the time," Stacy goes. I kick at the water bottle on the ground. It slides a little and then spins once, pointing toward Stacy. I sneak a glance at Tim, who looks like he did that time last month when we thought we were stuck in the elevator at the mall.

"Don't you want to kiss her?" Stacy asks Tim, like some kind of lawyer or something. Tim sort of shrugs.

"I don't know how," he finally says. Well, that's a relief.

Stacy flips her hair back over her shoulders, away from her face. "Come here," she goes to Tim.

"What for?"

"Just come here," she says again. Then she looks at me. "You watch."

Tim walks a few steps toward her. The mansion's roof is sagging, from the rain, I guess, and it nearly touches their heads.

"What?" Tim goes.

Stacy steps forward now and presses her whole body against his. She keeps one foot back to brace herself, and the next thing I know, she's got her hand behind his head and her mouth on his. She's not doing some little peck. No way. She's kissing him slow. Really slow. And then I see her mouth open a little, but somehow, it's not gross like it is on TV, with mashed lips all over the place, even though their tongues must be touching, silver ring and all. Something low in my stomach glides, and inside me, below my belly button, things start to melt. She kisses him and kisses him like that for a long, long time. And she doesn't finish fast, but kind of pulls her head away just enough so her mouth is barely touching his anymore, but almost. She stays like that a second, and then she pushes him away, sort of rough.

"That's how you do it," she says. The place underneath my belly slides again, and Tim's face is just as red as mine must be, and he stands there, really still. "Now you guys try it," Stacy goes. Tim and I don't move.

"What's the holdup here?" Simon calls, shoving his head and shoulders through the tent's entrance. "We're waiting on you!" He disappears again, and Stacy looks at Tim and me. She's aggravated.

"I guess Alex must like Simon better than you," she tells Tim.

"I do not!" I go.

"I thought you said *Simon* liked *Alex*," Tim goes.

Stacy shrugs and bends down to crawl out. "Maybe they like each other," she says with a smirk. I shake my head at Tim, to let him know that's just stupid, but he won't even look at me.

When it's time to leave, I get into Teddy's dad's van instead of Simon's car. I end up right next to Tim.

"I thought you were riding with Simon," he mutters.

"I thought you were," I go. We're quiet for a minute while some of the other kids climb in.

"So Stacy thinks you like him," Tim tells me. His voice breaks on *like*.

"What happened to her being full of it?" I go. Tim shrugs and looks out the window, toward the three pine trees in the distance. Teddy climbs in up front next to his dad, who guns the engine. "How was kissing her?" I go, trying to sound casual.

"Gross," he says. I think he's lying.

He looks at me. "What?" he asks.

"Nothing," I say, and when the van starts, he leans his forehead against the glass and doesn't talk the whole way home.

12

MY MOM ISN'T too happy about my cheek.

"Must have been a pretty sharp branch," she goes, tracing her thumb down the scab. She's wearing the pajamas I gave her for Mother's Day last year—pink silk top and bottoms. They look really good on her. Now she lifts my chin to get a closer look.

"It's not infected," she goes. "Does it hurt?"

"No," I say. "I told you. Simon put stuff on it right when it happened."

"I hope it doesn't scar." She frowns. "You have such a pretty face." My mother's never said anything like that before.

"Thanks," I go.

She kisses my good cheek. "You're welcome."

* * *

After she turns off the hall light, I sneak out of bed into the bathroom. I tip the toilet seat down, gentle, so it won't bang. Then I step up and face the mirror over the sink. And there I am. Just a regular twelve-year-old. Brown hair. Brown eyes. My good points are straight teeth that don't need braces and a winking dimple in my right cheek that I always forget about. My bad point is all the hair I don't have the patience to do anything with. My mother's always telling me to get the bangs out of my eyes.

Then there's my body. It's just regular too. Skinny, average height, and no curves anywhere. Actually, that's kind of a lie. If I turn sideways and pull my nightshirt close, small lumps poke out of my chest. They're little, but not a bad shape. Stacy's flatter than I am, even though she's older. Marie wears a bra, but her chest is sort of funny, more like tubes than bumps. The boys talk about her on the soccer field sometimes when they think I can't hear. Sophie has boobs too, but hers are perfect. Not too big and not too small. Not too pointy and not too round. Just right. Kind of like Baby Bear's porridge, I think, and I try not to laugh out loud, standing here on the toilet seat like some kind of maniac.

I'm hoping if you look hard enough, you can figure out if you're pretty or not. It's easy to tell with other people, but I want to know what I am. I want to know who Tim thinks is the best-looking girl in our class. Tim and I talk about a lot of things, but we've never talked about that. I wonder if he thinks of me as a real girl or not. I wonder if he would want to kiss me, now that he knows how. I don't want him to like kissing Stacy. And I don't want him to think I like Simon, either. I know Tim doesn't think Simon is nasty, like Stacy says. But it seems like maybe Tim thinks I'm the nasty one now.

I think it's my alarm going off, but then I figure out it's a beeper. I wait awhile, hearing the sounds of my parents whispering, shuffling out of bed, pulling open drawers. It's pitch black outside my window.

"Mom?" I go, sitting up. "Dad?"

My mother opens my bedroom door, letting in this patch of light from the hallway.

"It's okay, Alex," she goes. "Everything's okay."

"Is it that patient?" They don't usually get beeped in the middle of the night. And I can't remember the last time one of them actually had to go somewhere in the middle of the night either. "Is it that Martha patient?" My mom comes over and sits on the edge of my bed. She's got her toothbrush in her hand, the bristles all wet, and her breath smells like mint.

"Yes," she says. "She's in pretty bad shape. I'm going to the hospital to see what I can do."

"What time is it?"

"Four forty-five. Tim's father is sending over a taxi, so Dad will do breakfast with you and then drive in and meet me at the clinic later, okay?"

"Okay."

I expect her to stand up fast and rush out, but she sits there for a minute looking at me. It's nice.

"What?" I go, feeling shy all of a sudden.

"Nothing," my mom tells me.

"Ann?" my dad calls. "Taxi's here." She stands up.

"Coming," she calls back. She touches my hand. "Bye, sweetie."

My dad and I sleep through our alarms, so by the time I get to class, flash cards are over and everybody's working on something else. Tim's in the silent study room, at a table far from Stacy. He hasn't saved me a seat, like he usually does, and while I'm pretending not to notice, Simon calls over.

"Glad you could make it," he goes. I sit next to Teddy.

"Sorry," I tell Simon.

"Are you okay?" Teddy says.

"My cheek hurt," I lie. "My mother had to put stuff on it." Simon hears me and comes right over. He leans down and holds my chin in his hand, like my mom did last night. The minute he touches me, the whole class seems to know it. From all the way in the silent study room, both Stacy and Tim look over, and I can feel the other kids eyeing us too. Stacy must have been talking again this morning. I pull back fast.

"Sorry." Simon pulls his hand away. "Did that hurt?"

"A little." I can't look at him. I want to tell him to go away, to stop getting us into more trouble. He's making me mad with how stupid he is. He stands there for a second, like he wants to ask me something, but then he sort of looks around and then walks off. I want to go after him and explain somehow, but I can't. Everybody's watching. Everybody will take it the wrong way. My stomach churns. Teddy's staring at me.

"What?" I go. Teddy looks away. "It's not true!" I say. "None of what she says is true!" Teddy keeps his head down.

"That scrimmage with St. John's is coming up," Danny finally says, from the round table next to us. "The week after next. Simon told us before flash cards."

"Good," I say, swallowing something nasty that's come right up through my throat. "I plan on kicking ass."

At lunch, after stampeding through the playground to the soccer field, we all stop short. Our dirt patch is gone. Instead, like magic, there's a thick, green lawn.

"Oh yeah," Viv says. "We forgot." No mud, no holes, no

rocks. Those workmen are here again. Two of them are unrolling a long green strip. It unwinds flat, over the last bare section of soil, like the final swipe of fresh paint on an old wall.

"That's wild," Danny goes. "Is it real?"

"It's real all right," one of the men says. "Takes some time to settle in, so stay off it for a few days." Then he stamps his booted foot over a bump, leveling it out.

"Last one to the stream's second pick for all of next week!" Danny calls, taking off.

"Hey," Tim moans. "No fair!" And we're gone.

"Hold it!" Stacy goes as soon as we burst through the trees into the clearing. "Stop right there!"

"The soccer field's all new," Teddy puffs out, calling across the ladder to Stacy. "And we can't play on it yet."

"Don't you have to start practicing for your scrimmage?" Marie asks. She's sitting on the school side of the bank, on top of a book on top of a flat rock. I shrug and plunk myself down next to her. The ground is warm. So is the air. I take off my sweater.

"Probably we should," I go, "but missing a couple of days won't matter much." Even with everything that's happening, a wave of excitement washes over me. We'll be ready for St. John's. I just know it.

"We're going to build a tree house," Marie says. "Stacy's going to show us how."

"You don't know how to build a freaking tree house," Danny goes. He starts throwing rocks into the water.

"Shove it," Stacy tells him.

"Yeah," Sebastian goes. "Shove it." He's leaning on a boulder.

"She doesn't, man," Danny says.

Tim walks in my direction. Maybe he's finally going to talk to me. But he stops halfway over and just sits on the ground, all by himself. Viv drops down next to him. I can tell Stacy's staring at me. I can tell she doesn't like it that I won't talk to her now. She's going to try to make me.

"Alex," she says, "I rule on the ladder now. I've been practicing." Whatever. "Check me out," she calls, acting all innocent. And she starts leaping from rung to rung. She's not bad. Not like her first day, all wobbly and everything. This time she's got a good flow, and her feet are hitting the rungs solid, with light sneaker squeaks on the metal. But then suddenly it goes wrong.

One minute Stacy's bounding across, really graceful, hair flowing like some sort of scarf, and the next minute she's lying half in the stream and half on the bank. She's screaming. None of us moves at first, but then Tim and Viv and I are beside her, only I can't remember how we got there. Stacy's arm is twisted the wrong way, and there's a bone sticking out of it and blood everywhere.

"Marie," Viv goes, fast. "You go get Simon." Stacy's screaming like crazy. The blood. "Tim, you get Maggie to call an ambulance." Marie and Tim take off.

"Don't move, Stacy," Viv tells Stacy. "It'll be okay." She just keeps screaming long, high notes—the kind that break windows on TV shows. Her blood is everywhere. It's pouring out of her arm. She can't bleed so much. Not Stacy.

Viv turns to Teddy. "Give me your shirt," Viv goes. Teddy doesn't hesitate for even a second. He pulls his shirt over his head quick as anything. He knows what Viv is doing. We all do. We learned about it during Science Unit Eight. If someone's hurt, you're supposed to stop the bleeding, first thing.

Teddy and I help Viv wrap Stacy's arm. She screams one unbelievably loud, nightmare scream when we touch her. We wrap as tight as we can, right over that piece of bone, and when we're done, she goes quiet. Completely quiet, like she's asleep, only her eyes are open. She's so quiet, I can hear the stream tinkling, and all of us breathing heavy, and the sound of feet clomping on the ground behind me. It's Simon. Tim's not with him, and neither is Maggie.

Blood is already seeping through Teddy's shirt. "You have to stop the bleeding," I hear myself say.

"This is going to hurt bad, Stacy," Simon tells her. Even though she doesn't look like she's hearing anything, Simon keeps talking anyway. "You yell all you want," he says, pulling off his shirt. She doesn't even blink.

"Simon," I say, "don't let her bleed so much." He ties his shirt right over Teddy's. He does it fast. His smooth chest has beads of sweat on it. I watch one drip down to his belly button and then stay there, shuddering. Stacy moans a low, rumbling sound, like an angry dog. Simon lifts her up and starts running through the woods toward the school building. He reminds me of Tarzan, carrying Jane, with his bare top and Stacy limp in his arms. The rest of us follow. We run over blood. It sticks to the bottoms of our sneakers.

We rush into the lobby of the lower school behind Simon, just as the teachers are closing their doors to packs of little kids peeking out.

"An ambulance is on the way," Maggie says as Simon hurries Stacy into her office. "I called . . . ," and her voice fades to something I can't hear while Simon puts Stacy on the floor back there and leans over her. Maggie steps out, closing her office door behind her. "Back to your classroom immediately," she orders us.

"She's bleeding too much," I try to tell her. I guess I must be yelling because the other kids look at me funny, and Maggie kneels down.

"She'll be okay, Alex," Maggie goes. "They'll give her new blood at the hospital."

"No," I say. It's hard to talk. It's hard for me to get the words out. They're too important. "She'll bleed to death!" Where's Tim? "Maggie, she's not allowed—" Maggie puts her hands on my shoulders.

"Nobody's going to let her bleed to death." She tightens her grip on me. "See?" she says, nodding toward the double doors. Her fingers are digging into my skin through my T-shirt. "Here's the ambulance now."

Two paramedics swoop in with a gurney and emergency kits and things. But Maggie doesn't know, and Tim's not here to help me explain, and nobody's listening anyway. I might not like her, but I can't just let Stacy die.

Simon bangs out of Maggie's office. "She's in shock," he whispers. I yank out of Maggie's grip. The paramedics run right past Simon into the office and close the door again. "From the sound of things out here," Simon goes, "seems like Alex might be close to it too."

"I'm not in shock!" I say loud. I'm about to try to explain everything again, but the words never come out because right then another man bursts through the double doors. He's huge, and even under his business suit and shiny shoes, you can tell he has muscles like some kind of professional wrestler or something. He walks fast, straight toward us, and he looks pissed off. He blows right by me, knocking my shoulder and nearly shoving me to the ground in his hurry. He doesn't even notice.

"I'm Reade Janice," he booms. "Where's my daughter?"

I burst into tears before I even know why, and it isn't until I'm alone outside that I realize it's because that's Stacy's father, and she's the biggest liar I've ever known.

I've been sitting on top of the jungle gym forever, staring up at the newly fuzzed soccer field and trying to stop crying. I hear steps behind me, but I don't have the energy to turn around. Then the jungle gym sways a little with the weight of someone heavy, and Simon is here, swinging his legs right next to mine. He's wearing a fresh shirt. I wonder where he got it. His hands still have blood on them, and so do his pants, just like mine.

We don't say anything for a while. I want to put my head on his shoulder because I'm so tired, but I can't because of Stacy's lies, and that makes me mad and sad, and I want to cry again. I wish things were like they used to be.

"Never saw you so upset," Simon finally says. "You scared the daylights out of me." He's waiting for an answer.

"Where's Tim?" I go.

"I think he's still throwing up in the bathroom," he says. He drums his fingers on the metal bars, which are sort of hot from the sun.

"She told me her father was dead," I try to explain. My voice sounds strange, kind of like there's no person behind it. "She told me that they were Jehovah's Witnesses and that he died because he couldn't have a blood transfusion." I feel myself blush with the embarrassment from having believed it. Simon stops swinging his legs.

"That was a whopper," he goes. We get quiet again, and then I decide I may as well see if Simon can help.

"I wish I could figure out why she lies so much," I say.

"People are complicated," he goes. "Seems to me, when someone tells that kind of lie, the kind Stacy fed you . . . Well, there's usually some truth hidden in it somewhere."

"Huh?" I say. "I don't get it." How could any part of that lie be true? Am I supposed to think Stacy's dad really was in some car wreck? Or that they really are Jehovah's Witnesses? He wasn't. I just know he wasn't. And they're not. It was a lie. Every stupid bit of it. And so is every single thing Stacy's ever said.

"Even if the content of someone's lie seems like it's a pure lie," Simon says, "there may be something real in it somewhere. Sometimes it's the reason for the lie that gives us a clue as to where the truth is."

"Well, I don't care about any reasons," I say, and I'm so mad all over again. "I couldn't care less."

"But there is a reason," Simon says. "And someone who tells a lie like that probably needs a friend more than most other people do."

"I don't want to be her friend," I go. "She's not a good person, Simon."

"I'm sure she's not a bad person either."

"I thought she was going to die," I tell him. Then I'm crying again. Simon pulls me into a sideways hug and lets me mess up his second shirt of the day. When I stop, resting my chin on his shoulder, I finally see Tim, standing at the edge of the playground, watching us. I move back from Simon fast, but Tim's already jogging away.

You'd think I'd want to cry all over again, knowing what he must still be thinking about Simon and me, but I don't. Or maybe I can't. Nothing that happens anymore seems right, and I'm tired of wanting it to be.

13

I WALK STRAIGHT home from the jungle gym, even though the school day isn't over. Simon doesn't think it's a good idea, but he can't stop me either.

When I let myself in through the back door, my father's toeing off his shoes.

"What are you doing here?" I go, helping myself to a Hostess box from our pantry.

"Same thing you are." He drops his briefcase to the floor. "Skipping." He swings a chair away from the kitchen table to straddle it, backward. "Simon and Maggie called me at work," he explains. "I wanted to be here when you got home."

"Mom couldn't leave the clinic, right?" I slip a cupcake out of its plastic wrapping right onto the kitchen table. If my mother were here, she'd tell me to use a napkin.

"Actually, she was still at the hospital when I got the call," my father goes. The frosting has white corkscrew swirls, like an old telephone cord, dividing it down the center.

"With that Martha, right?" I say. He doesn't really answer.

"I called Mom there," he goes, "and she checked everything out." He rests his elbows on the table. "Stacy's going to be okay."

"Did she have to have a blood transfusion?"

"I don't know."

"If she needed one, would she have died if they couldn't have given it to her?"

"She might have died in a situation like that," my dad says. "But she's fine." I pick the frosting from the top of my cupcake. It peels off like a chocolate sticker.

"She said she couldn't have blood transfusions," I go. "I thought they would let her die."

"Yeah," my dad goes. "Simon told me that's what you thought." He watches me pull the cupcake apart and lick out the whipped sugar center. "He also said you were right there when it happened," he goes. "And that you were pretty scared."

"Here." I hold out the other half of the cupcake. "You can have the rest."

"Alex," he goes, like he's about to ask me a question. He takes the cupcake.

"Yeah?"

He stares at me a minute and then pops my gift into his mouth. He barely even chews before it's gone. "Maybe you'll visit her. Talk things out."

"No." She made me feel so dumb. And all those lies about Simon. And about me. My father looks like he's waiting for something.

"You can't talk things out with her," I try to explain. "Besides, there's nothing to talk out. I just don't like her."

"Because she lied to you about her religion and her father dying?" He's got chocolate on his tooth.

"That. And other lies. Like about Simon. She says the worst stuff about Simon." My father might really know what to do. I could tell him about it. Tell him everything. Even though it's so embarrassing. Even though it's the kind of thing you don't want to go around talking to your father about. I could tell him right now. But he starts up again.

"Remember that time Mom asked you about the thief?"

"Yeah," I say. "She was really talking about Martha." My dad nods. "Is Mom going to help her live longer and then send her to jail?"

"She's going to try to help Martha live longer," my dad says. "And she doesn't want Martha to go to jail."

"But Martha's a thief and a drug addict and a liar," I say, "who doesn't treat her kids right or something."

"Your mother's struggling with how to make sense of and how to respond to a complex person acting in complex ways." I think I know what's coming. "Just like you're doing with Stacy." I knew it. "It's a struggle we all face at one time or another in our lives. It's especially a struggle if you're someone who cares."

"What do you mean, someone who cares?" I ask.

"I mean someone who wants to be a decent human being."

"Stacy's not a decent human being," I say. "And if Simon knew the stuff she was saying, he'd think that too."

"Simon can take care of himself," my dad says. "And you don't have to like someone every minute of the day to be their friend."

"I don't want to be her friend," I go. And then I don't say anything else. Because I don't want my father to think I'm not a decent human being.

After a while he pulls me and my chair out a little bit from the table, the way a waiter does for people at the end of a meal, so I stand up. "You're really angry with Stacy right now," my dad says, guiding me to the stairs. "But it's important to be fair to people. To give them second chances. If you give her another chance, I'm sure things can be patched up."

"I don't want to patch things up," I say. And then I start crying again. He hugs me, right there on the seventh stair.

"You want to lie down?" he goes, after I've pulled myself together.

"I'm not tired," I say, and then I feel like I'm three years old again because that's what I used to say when my parents made me take naps.

"You've had a rough day," my dad says. "Why don't you just lie down and see if you can sleep a little?"

"It's only one thirty," I say.

"True." Somehow, he ends up getting me to bed. It's warm out, but my dad covers me anyway. The next thing I know, it's morning.

I glance around for Tim when I'm tossing stuff into my locker, but he hasn't saved me a seat. I press on my stomach with my hand, hoping I can massage away the ache, and find a spot next to Sophie.

"Stacy's going to be okay," she goes. "She just broke her arm really bad."

"I know," I go. "My parents told me."

"Her mother and father threatened to sue the school," Sophie whispers. "My mom told them we don't have any money anyway."

"Great," I go.

"Yeah," she says. "Plus, now they're taking the ladder away. My mom says it's too dangerous." Then Sophie puts her hand on my arm. "You and Tim should make up."

"We're not in a fight," I say.

"Yes, you are."

I hang out with Teddy all day. We do math on the floor in the side hallway kitchen, leaning our backs against the oven. I don't know how we end up there, but I'm glad, because it keeps us away from everybody else.

"Everything under control back here?" Simon wants to know, poking his head around the corner to check on us, right before lunch.

"Yeah," we say.

"Teddy," Simon goes, "leave us be a minute."

"Is Alex in trouble?" Teddy goes.

"No."

Teddy looks at me funny, like he doesn't believe Simon. "Hope not," he tells me, and then he leaves.

I'm already nervous. I don't want Tim to see us and think I asked to be alone with Simon.

"What's up?" Simon goes.

"What do you mean?"

He leans against the kitchen counter and crosses one

ankle over the other. "Are we all right?" he goes. "You and me?"

"Uh-huh."

"Because you seemed sort of upset again when you took off yesterday."

"Uh-uh," I go.

"If there's anything more we need to talk about, we can, you know." But how am I supposed to tell him Stacy claims he's a pervert and has Tim and maybe everybody else believing I *like* him? "Something's going on with you." He doesn't sound mad or anything, just kind of confused. "Yesterday was the first talk we've had in a while. It wasn't such a long talk, either."

"I was upset yesterday," I go. He looks so bummed.

"Yep." He nods. "Me too." I hate how worried he seems. I hate that things are so different between us. I want to fix it, to make things right again. But I can't think of what to say. "That latrine thing still on your mind?" He's looking at me really steady. I blush and shake my head. We stay there a minute, but then Simon unhooks his ankles. "Hope you're getting ready for the game next week," he goes.

I am.

Time passes sort of slow, but somehow, even with all the weirdness, a bunch of days go by. The next thing I know, we're pulling up to St. John's in Teddy's dad's van, only it's Teddy's mom who's driving this time. Tim has brand-new cleats.

"Sweet," I try, just to see if he'll talk to me for a change. He won't.

"Oh man," Danny goes, when we pull up to their field. The St. John's team has blue-and-gold uniforms. Plus, they're in these complicated formations, passing and shooting into a real goal: white posts, a yellow net, and all. They look professional almost. We don't look like anything. Even with our sixth and seventh graders, we barely have enough players. Plus, we don't have actual uniforms. Just white shirts, red shorts, and cleats. My cleats are sort of old, but I like them that way. Worn in and soft.

We trickle out onto the field and try to act like we've done this before. And then I kind of see us the way other people probably do—the way Stacy must have seen us on her first day. We're all different sizes and colors, and we're sort of sloppy-looking, and we have a girl on our team. My heart starts to pound, and even with everything that's happened, I'm psyched because I know they don't expect me to be as good as the guys.

Simon talks to the St. John's coach at the sidelines for a minute and then gathers us in a circle. "We've got the kickoff," he goes. "Remember, their best player is their right wing. They think Alex is our weak link. Take advantage of that. Okay?"

"Okay," we say.

"Good." Simon raises his voice. "Most important thing?"

"Have fun!" we go.

"Play ball!" Simon yells, and we break out onto the field.

On the whistle Tim tips the ball over to Danny, who passes back to Viv. At left wing I'm already racing forward, wide open. Their defense isn't even watching. Viv arcs the ball to me. Even after I trap it, their guys don't look worried. They dive in too fast, and I dribble around them, easy, set up a shot, and smack the ball. It glides into the air, floats into the goal at the top right-hand corner, and falls for the score. Less than ten seconds into the half. Beautiful.

The St. John's guys are pissed. "Who's covering her?" one of them shouts, angry.

"Come on, John's!" their coach yells. "That was a *girl*!"

"Luck," their right wing mutters.

I don't care about any of that until Tim won't slap five with me. He pretends he has a gnat in his eye all the way until the next whistle. Then he passes off to Danny again, who sends it right back to him for a give-and-go.

"Tim!" I yell. "Man on!" Two St. John's guys are chasing him down from behind.

"Give it to Alex!" Viv calls. Instead, Tim boots the ball to Viv, who loses it because his St. John's guy has him covered tight now.

"Tim, man," Danny says, mad. "What's wrong? Nobody's taking Alex! She's wide open!" Tim spits on the grass and shoves his hair out of his eyes.

It goes like that for a long time. St. John's starts to cover me better after a while because I score another goal, no thanks to Tim. He won't play with me. He won't pass, he won't set me up, he won't do anything. Finally, after their striker scores his third goal, tying the game, Simon calls a time-out.

"What the hell's going on out there?" he goes, thumping Tim on the head and glaring at me, like I'm to blame too.

"Ask him," I go. My voice is high and shaky. I bite my lip, hating it.

"Timothy?" Simon goes.

"Nothing's wrong," Tim says.

"Right," Danny mutters.

"Keep your squabbles off the field," Simon warns. But Tim won't pass to me the whole rest of the game. I don't score again, even though Viv and one of our seventh graders do, and we win; 5–3.

I make sure I'm behind Tim when it's time for handshakes. We form a moving line with the St. John's players in the middle of the field to give lazy sideways hand slaps and mutter, "Game, game, game," like a chant.

"You ruined it," I hiss at Tim's back, near the end of the line. He doesn't even turn around. Just heads for the van. He ruined the whole thing.

14

TIM'S SITTING ON the curb with his back to me, waiting for his mom to pick him up. All the other kids are gone, and Simon's gaining speed out of the parking lot on his bike. The side of my leg hurts, where a St. John's guy fouled me, and a little piece of the scab on my cheek is oozing, but I'm too mad to feel any of that.

"Tim," I say to his back. I wait, figuring he'll answer me, now that we're alone, but he doesn't move. "What's wrong with you?" I go. There's a big green-and-brown smear on his T-shirt from when he did a slide tackle at the end of the game. He swivels his head toward the parking lot entrance, where it sounds like there might be a car turning in, but it's a false alarm. "Timothy!" I yell. He picks up a bunch of pebbles and snaps one out a few feet—almost like he's trying to make it skip, only there's no water. All of a sudden, I'm practically running over to him, and he's jumping up, twisting and backing away from me all at once. I shove him.

"What are you doing?" he goes.

"Why didn't you pass?" I want to hit him. In the face.

"You know why."

"I do not." My hands are all balled up, like I might really punch him. He smashes the rest of his stones on the ground. One of them sprays up to sting my ankle.

"You like Simon."

"So do you," I go.

"Not the way you do!"

"Stacy told you that!"

"So?"

"Stacy makes up a lot of crap," I go. "You know she does."

"I saw you hugging him," Tim says. "Stacy didn't make that up."

"I've seen you hug him too. So what?"

"That's different."

"How?" He doesn't answer. "How is that different?" Somehow, I've moved forward even more, and he has to tilt his neck to keep my face out of his.

"Stacy said you told her you like him. She said you didn't want to kiss me because you like kissing him more."

"I never said that!" I hate her. Tim won't look at me now. I lower my voice. "That's disgusting, and I never did that, and I never said that."

"You saw his dick," Tim accuses, like I must have wanted to or something.

"By accident," I go.

"Stacy said you guys were touching and stuff that night in the tent."

"We were asleep," I say. "And Stacy knows it. And he's old, Tim." Now he's looking at me. "He's too old."

"They like younger women," Tim goes.

I don't understand. "Who?" I ask.

Tim swallows and bends down to gather more stones. He tosses them at my cleats. "Older men," he mutters. "Older men like younger women."

"Who told you that?" I ask. "Stacy?" Tim nods, flicking his wrist at my feet. I snort.

"Well, other people say it too," Tim goes. "I've even heard my parents talk about it." I feel the little rocks bouncing off my toes, the sides of my foot, my instep. "Everybody knows it, Alex. Come on."

"Well, I don't know about other people," I say, "but I know Simon. And so should you. He's not some older man. He's just Simon. And I'm not a woman. I'm just a girl."

"Then why were you two hugging yesterday?" He doesn't sound mad anymore. Instead, he sounds like he's about to cry.

"I don't know." How do you describe things you do that come out of a feeling? How do you make one feeling sound okay, when others aren't? "I was upset, and he was just trying to make me feel better." Tim's chin is all trembly. "I don't like him like that," I say loud and strong. "I swear." He's run out of things to throw. His hands dangle by his sides. I hear a car pulling in from Maple Avenue to the parking lot, and I know it's going to be his mother. "Stacy says weird things," I go. Tim nods a little nod. "We can't let her mess us up like that."

"You're the one who wanted to be her friend so bad," Tim goes.

"Just in the very beginning," I say. "Besides, you're the one who kissed her."

"I did not kiss her!" His mom's car circles and slows. "She kissed me."

"Well, you liked it." I'm hoping he'll deny it. But maybe he doesn't have time because his mom's car is coming to a stop right next to us.

"Anyway," he goes, "it was a good game."

"You should have passed to me, moron," I tell him.

"Sorry."

His mom lowers the passenger window. "Hi, guys."

"We won," Tim and I tell her. Then we slap five. Friends again.

"Of course you did." She smiles through her long curls. Her hair is just like Tim's. "Want a ride, Alex?" she asks.

In the backseat I feel more tired than I ever felt before in my life. The world blurs by through the window, and Tim and his mom's conversation up front turns into a murmur without words. My body is tired, and my brain is tired, and then somehow, my mind goes all the way back to when I was in the lower school, to how I learned to read. My teacher gave me these small squares of paper, each coated with a sandpaper letter. I had to trace the sandpaper over and over with my fingertips until I got the feel of how that same shape might ease out from a pencil. I remember tracing the whole alphabet for weeks, not understanding that it was language under my touch, just winding lines scraping my fingertips. And then one day those lines turned into letters, and the letters turned into *cat* and *pot* and *straw*, and I could read. I could figure out the world.

I want things to make sense now, but there aren't any tricks to help me. I can't trace paper for what I don't understand anymore. The things I need to figure out don't have rules. Like why Stacy wants it to be true that Simon and I like each other in that certain way. Like why I've been scared sometimes lately that maybe she's right. What if Simon does look at me? What if he did want me to see his thing? What if that slow, sliding feeling I've been getting lately is because I like him? Most of me knows it can't be, but then why am I suddenly restless sometimes, in the middle of the night or at school, or even on the soccer field? Why do I want to feel something light, maybe on the arm or on the lips, and how come, even though I think it was an accident that time Simon touched my chest, I can't get it out of my mind?

One time last year Simon found out that Marie was doing the same math workbook over and over again. Simon couldn't figure out why Marie would do that, and when he asked, Marie said it was because it was easy—because she knew how to do those problems. Then Simon told Marie that once you figure one thing out, you're supposed to move on to the next thing, and that's the way to grow in the world. And then Marie had started to cry, and she kept saying, "But I don't want to move on! I know how to do *this*!"

I didn't get it then, but now I do. I don't want to move on either. Everything's too hard, too complicated, and I want to stay right where I am—or maybe where I was—where it's easy.

15

IT'S DARK, AND I'm still wiped out from the game and everything, and my mother and I have been driving a long time to find Stacy's street. Just when I'm feeling better, thinking that maybe we really won't find it after all, my mom perks up.

"Park Place!" she goes. "Here it is." She turns right. "Start looking at numbers." I don't answer. "102, 104, 106 . . ." My mom's driving slow so she won't miss 114. She pulls to a stop in front of a long driveway with a smashed metal mailbox leaning crazily off its green post. She lifts a package of chocolates and a bunch of flowers from the seat between us into my lap. I don't move. "Alex, stop this right now."

"Stop what?"

"I know she lied to you about her father," my mom

says for the millionth time. "I know she embarrassed and scared you with that lie. But you have to learn to forgive people."

"Why?" I sound obnoxious, but I couldn't care less.

"Because, Alex," my mom says, "it's the right thing. The fair thing."

"It's not fair to lie," I say.

My mom sighs. "No, it's not," she says. "But people do lie to us, and we have to figure out how to know the truth for ourselves or how to handle it when we can't do that. We have to look at the facts of things, at all sides of things. Including all sides of people's lies."

"Whatever," I say.

"Drop the attitude, Alex," my mom says. "Stacy needs to heal. And people heal with the concern, support, and understanding of friends."

She's never lectured me like this before. It feels like she's reading from a recipe or something. Where's the mom from that time in the middle of the night? The one who really looked at me? Nowhere.

She's waiting for me to answer her.

"She only broke her arm," I finally say.

"Badly," my mom answers. "She's in a lot of pain." *So am I,* I want to shout. *Inside somewhere.* "They're expecting you,

Alex," my mom says. "I told Stacy's mother you'd be here at eight o'clock. I'll be back in half an hour. Now go."

I get out of the car and slouch across Stacy's driveway to a brick walk that winds its way to a small front porch. There's a light there with moths swirling around it, like a sloppy soccer team fighting for a loose ball. I knock on the front door, hoping nobody will answer, but then Stacy's mom swings it open. She's small with big eyes, like Stacy, only she blinks a lot.

"You must be Alex," she says.

"Yeah," I mutter.

"Thank you for coming," she goes. She says it all formal, stiff. "I'll get Stacy." Then she just walks away without even inviting me inside. Weird.

"Stace!" I hear her call once. I hear Stacy's footsteps, and then she's here, with practically her whole arm inside a thick orange cast held up with a blue sling and her hair spreading over her shoulders.

"Are those for me?" she asks right away, looking at the flowers and box of chocolates. I nod. Stacy steps out and shuts the door behind her. She lowers herself to the top step, careful of her arm. I see her wince when she moves. I guess she is in a lot of pain. "Sit," she goes. I sit next to her and shove the gifts into her lap. But not too hard. "Thanks," she goes. Her tongue ring's gone. Maybe they made her take it out in the hospital. Maybe doctors think tongue rings are unsanitary or something.

"They're not from me," I say. I swat away the flying beetles that can't get in on the moths' game. "They're from my parents. They made me come."

"I have to tell you something." She lowers her voice. "It's important, and I wanted to call you, but my mom's been nearby the whole time, so I couldn't." Stacy rips open the plastic shrink-wrap off the chocolate box. She's still wincing, but it's not stopping her from getting to that candy.

"I thought you didn't have a father!" I tell her. "I thought you were going to die!"

"Yeah." She nods, picking through the assortment. "Sorry about that."

"You're sorry?"

She bites into a chocolate, drops it back into its paper cup, and then chooses another one. "I didn't think you really believed that Jehovah's Witness stuff," she goes. "Nobody else would have."

"A lot of people believe what you say!"

"If you're talking about Tim," she says, "I had to change the truth around a little for him. It's better that way." She holds the candy box out to me with her good arm. I ignore it.

"What's that supposed to mean?" I think about just

getting up and walking home. The thing is, we're pretty far from my house. And it's dark out. Plus, my mom's supposed to pick me up.

"God," Stacy moans. She picks out another candy and bites into it. Cherry drips down her chin. "The truth about Simon is, he *is* a pervert, only Tim doesn't want to hear that because Simon's like some kind of father to him or something. So Simon has to be perfect, or else Tim will freak out. So it was just easier to tell him that what's going on is that you have a crush on Simon. Not the other way around." She swallows and wipes her chin with her finger. "So, see, I was protecting Tim from the truest truth because he couldn't handle it."

"But there's nothing going on," I say. "Nothing. You're wrong, Stacy. Simon's not a pervert, and nothing is going on."

She slaps the chocolate box on the ground and jams her face in mine. "I am not wrong!"

I jump up, knocking her stupid candy off the steps. Chocolates and little paper cups scatter everywhere. "I don't listen to liars!" I yell. Her mouth gets thin. "And you don't scare me anymore, Stacy, so don't even try it!" I pound down the steps to the brick walk. I'll walk home. Far or not. Dark or not.

"Alex," she says to my back.

"Screw you!" I don't even turn around. "Liar!" I'm almost to the driveway before I hear her running.

"I'm not making it up," she pants out behind me. "Alex, wait." I keep going, fast. She catches up. "Alex, I swear." She huffs. We're on her driveway now. "Okay," she admits, "I have sort of lied before." I stop. There's just enough light coming from the houses and street lamps that I can see her expression, the glimmer from her cast, the black space between her white front teeth. "I'm sorry about the thing with my father," she goes. "That was a lie. It was."

"Why did you tell it?" I say. "Just explain why."

She tosses her head like a pony. "I wanted to pretend he was dead." I can't imagine wanting to pretend something like that. "And . . . I don't know why else. I don't know."

"I bet it's not even true that Jehovah's Witnesses can't get blood transfusions," I say. Then I start walking again. She walks along with me. Her face is all scrunched up.

"That part was true," she goes. "I saw it on TV. That's really true, and what I have to tell you is true, and you have to listen." She stamps her foot hard. Then she starts to cry. I'm so surprised, I stop short. I never thought I'd see Stacy cry over anything. She uses her good hand to swipe at her eyes and then push on them to keep the tears in.

"Okay," I say. To give her a chance. To be fair. "I'm listening. What?"

It takes her a few seconds. A car drives by slow, its

headlights shining on us long enough for me to notice the cherry stain on Stacy's shirt and the pale yellow hospital bracelet on her good arm. "When I fell . . . ," she finally starts. "When Simon took me into Maggie's office . . ."

"What?'"

"He messed with me in there."

"Huh?"

"He touched me," she whispers. "He touched me and stuff."

"Nuh-uh," I go.

"You can't tell anyone," she warns. "You better not. But you're alone with him a lot, aren't you? And he likes you, Alex. He does." She's talking fast now. "That's why I had to tell you. So you can be careful."

"I don't believe you."

"I swear, Alex. He was doing stuff to me in there."

"What stuff?" I go. "What did he do, exactly?"

"You can't tell anyone. My father will kill him. You saw my father."

"What did Simon do?" I ask again, because I can't imagine it, really. What people do.

"Look," Stacy says. "I like you, Alex. And I don't want him to mess with you, too. That's all."

"I don't believe you," I tell her.

"Don't be mad," she goes. "Please, Alex. Don't be mad I told you, but it's true."

"Why would he touch you if he liked me?" I ask, and then I feel my face flush because that sounds like I'm jealous or something.

"Because he's a pervert, Alex!" She stamps her foot again. "You are so stupid! Don't you get it? He's a pervert!"

"Then you ought to tell your parents," I go. "If it really happened, you ought to tell them." She marches over to her mailbox sticking out of the ground, leaning lopsided to one side and smashed up in the back. It's gleaming in the night light like some sort of metal skeleton.

"My father did that!" She's pointing at the mailbox and yelling at me now. "With his bare hands! My father's crazy! He'll kill Simon if he finds out! He'll kill him!"

"I'm going home." I break into a run.

"You better not tell," she yells after me. "You better not, unless you want Simon killed!"

I keep running until I can't hear the sound of her voice anymore, and I keep on running after that. Headlights hit my eyes, blinding me for a second, and then I can see again, and it's my mother, on her way to pick me up.

"What happened?" She throws open her door and rushes over to me. I'm too out of breath to answer. "Alex, what's going on?" I push past her into the passenger seat. My mother drops into her place behind the steering wheel a second later. "Are you all right?" I lean my head against the window, the way Tim did riding home from our camping trip. The glass is cool against my skin. "Alex!" my mother goes.

"I'm fine," I say. "We had a fight, that's all."

"What do you mean?" my mother asks. "What happened?"

I shake my head. "Nothing," I say. "Nothing happened."

16

"NO WAY." TIM'S voice shatters on *way*. "Simon's not like that. He wouldn't do that."

We're a few feet from the edge of the woods, hidden from Maple Avenue for the first time in months by layers and layers of new spring leaves. Tim knew something was wrong last night when I called, asking him to meet me before school, but he didn't know exactly how bad things were.

"She tried to make me promise not to tell anyone," I say.

"She's insane," Tim goes. "I don't believe it."

"She was crying so hard," I whisper, even though there's nobody around to hear.

"So? What's that supposed to mean?"

"I don't know," I say. But I'm thinking about what Simon

told me: *Even if the content of someone's lie seems like it's a pure lie, there may be something real in it somewhere.*

"You don't believe it, do you?" The way his voice sounds makes me think that if I said I did, he might. Which fires up my stomach, because if he's that close to believing what Stacy's told me, then maybe I am too.

It's the reason for the lie that gives us a clue as to where the truth is.

"No, I don't believe it!" I say. We stand there for a second, and I get this urge to brush those curls out of Tim's eyes. I don't, though. Instead, I start walking.

"Maybe we ought to tell Simon what's going on," Tim says as we push out of the wood path and onto Maple Avenue's shoulder. Even though it's barely May, it's hot already. My underarms are damp.

"But what if Simon calls Stacy's parents?" I go. I'm thinking of that crumpled mailbox. Stacy might be a liar, but she didn't make that mailbox up. I saw it with my own eyes. Her father really could be crazy, if he did that.

"Maybe we could tell our parents," Tim goes. We cross the road and turn into the school driveway, which is pretty now, with dogwood trees all blooming pink and white.

"But they would call Stacy's, right?"

Tim nods. "Yeah. Probably."

"And then Stacy's dad might freak out anyway." I think about it. "He could hurt Simon." We're on the slate path, and we slow down. "I'll tell him," I decide.

"Really?"

"Yeah." I stare at the double doors and think about fairness. "Simon should know what she's saying about him. He has a right to know. You can't tell him because Stacy didn't tell you. She told me. So I'll do it."

"When?"

"I don't know." We push through the doors, and I see Stacy sitting at the round table with some of my mother's flowers stuck in her cast. She doesn't look so good. Her hair seems sort of stringy or something. She looks over at us and puts her one good hand on her hip. She knows I told Tim. I cross my arms over my chest and glare right back at her.

"She looks weird," Tim whispers.

"Who cares," I say. But she does look weird. Tired. Really tired. And something else. Something creepy.

I get my chance at lunch.

"Games day this afternoon," Simon announces. "And McDonald's for lunch." Everybody cheers.

"I call going with Simon!" Danny yells.

"Actually," Teddy says, "you went last time. It's my turn." He shrugs. "But you can go if you want."

"It's Stacy's turn," Simon goes. "She's never gone."

"I don't want to," Stacy goes. "My arm hurts."

I can talk to him in the car. "Let me go," I say. "I want to." The whole class gets really quiet. Has Stacy gotten to them already? She snorts. Soft, so Simon won't hear.

Maggie loans us her car while she covers our class for Simon. It has seats you stick to if you're sweaty. I start sticking right away. It's too hot for spring. It feels like July, or something. I have to keep unpeeling my thighs, almost before we're even out of the parking lot. Simon tries the air conditioner, but it doesn't work so well. We just roll down the windows instead.

"So," Simon says. Then he stops. Then he goes, "Are you okay?" I'm huddled up against my door.

"Yeah," I go, and I'm telling myself to spaz down so I can think of how to begin. But it's too hard. I can't relax. The ride to McDonald's is too short. I'll tell him on the way back, after I've had a chance to figure out how to say it. That's what I'll do.

We pull into McDonald's and park. I get out fast. I want to get inside, to the air-conditioning.

"You have the order list?" Simon asks me.

"Yeah," I say. Another voice overlaps with mine.

"Simon!" It's high and loud, like a cheerleader's. I look around. So does Simon. He smiles.

"Dawn," he goes to this girl wearing a short skirt, a tank top, and a blue jewel in her belly button. "What are you doing here?"

"Excellent," this Dawn girl goes. Simon laughs, and so does she.

"I'll meet you inside, okay?" he says to me.

"Okay," I say.

The air-conditioning blasts my skin as soon as I step through the doors. It's crowded, but the line moves fast. I'm wondering who Dawn is and how Simon can stand to stay out in the parking lot for so long with it so hot out. I look behind me every now and then, expecting him to come inside, but I don't see him.

"May I take your order, please?" the McDonald's lady asks me.

"Yeah," I say, looking one last time for Simon. "This is to go." I read our list to her. It's long, but she doesn't seem like she cares. She rings up the cash register and totals everything. Simon's got everybody's cash. I look around for him again, but he's still not here.

"I'll be back in a minute," I tell the McDonald's lady,

after she puts the first bag filled with fries on the counter. "I have to get the money from my teacher."

"Your teacher?" she goes, like there's something wrong with that, and she lifts her eyebrows. It doesn't help.

The parking lot's empty of people. The heat smothers me immediately, like plastic wrap stuck all over my body. Simon isn't anywhere. Maybe he came inside, and I just didn't see him. Maybe he sat at a table, waiting for me to get the food. I walk back in and then get goose bumps from the cold. I look around at all the tables. Simon's not there. Maybe he went into the bathroom. I stand by the men's room, waiting for him to come out. Then I get worried that all the food's ready and that lady is waiting for me to pay. If I'm not there, she might start putting the food back again. I go back to the counter. The McDonald's lady has three bags done, but she's still getting drinks, so I go back to the bathroom. A man comes out.

"Is there anyone else in there?" I ask him. He looks at me funny and shakes his head. Maybe Simon was in there when I went to check the counter just now, and then he walked out to the parking lot again. So I go back to the parking lot.

I almost miss him, except for this movement. This flicker. From a silver Bug, with its engine on and the windows rolled up. It's Simon in the front seat, practically on top of Dawn. Kissing her. With his hand on her chest over her shirt. Tongues. Belly button. That warm, sliding feeling.

Dawn pulls her head away suddenly, noticing me. I see her face again. She's younger than him. My stomach turns to stone. Way younger. I back up quick through the McDonald's door into the air-conditioning. There's a film of sweat all over me, but I'm shivering, too. I walk to the counter.

"You're holding up the line," the McDonald's lady complains.

"My teacher's coming with the money," I tell her. She raises her eyebrows again, and then Simon's behind me. He pays and takes the receipt. I grab three big bags, which is all I can manage, and Simon takes the drink trays and two more bags. I walk ahead of him out the door to Maggie's car. I don't see that silver Bug anywhere. *They like younger women.*

Simon rests the drink trays on the roof of the car and opens the back door.

"That was my friend Dawn," he tells me. I hand him my bags, and he puts them on the seat. *Older men like younger women.*

"Oh," I say.

"She works nearby." *Perverts.*

"Oh," I say again. I wonder what kind of work she does

dressed like that. I bet she doesn't work in any office. She didn't look old enough to be someone who works in an office.

Simon hands the drink trays to me. I put them on the floor of the backseat. They can't fall so easily back there.

"Actually," Simon says, "she's my girlfriend." We get into the car. It's about ten degrees hotter in here than outside.

"I guess you saw us, huh?" he goes. Did they plan it? Did they plan to meet in the McDonald's parking lot to fool around?

"Yeah," I say.

"I'm sorry," he goes. We're driving now, and even the wind on my face is hot, like a hair dryer.

"It doesn't matter," I say. "It's not like I haven't seen that before." I don't tell him I've only seen it on TV and at the movies.

"Is that right?" he says.

"Yeah," I go. I wish he would just drop it. I wish he would drive faster. I pretend to be really into the view out the window, so I won't have to look at him.

But all I can see is his mouth on hers and his hand on her chest over her shirt, and I can't help it, can't help feeling that melting, and my face is hot, and he's looking at me, all worried, and right then I think I might cry, and I try really hard not to, but my eyes fill up, and even though I blink hard, one big stupid fat tear gets out and spills down my face, and Simon sees it, and I want to die.

"Hey," he goes, all nice and everything. "Alex." He puts his hand on my leg. "I'm sorry." The flat of his hand on my leg. On my thigh. "I'm really sorry." And it stays there for a second, because I let it, because of the picture of that same hand on her chest over her shirt and the blue jewel and the skin and that soft sliding feeling and older men liking younger women—*Lech*—and then I pull away so fast, my knee slams hard into the door, and then Simon snatches his hand back and swerves a little bit on the road.

"Oh," he goes. "I . . ." But he doesn't finish.

It's quieter than anything after that. Not the kind of quiet that used to be so okay between us, though. It's that bad quiet. Ugly and thick.

"Didn't mean to upset you," Simon tells me finally.

"I'm not upset," I say. Because he was just touching my thigh to make me feel better. He was just touching it in a hug sort of a way, not some other gross way.

"I sure didn't mean to be disrespectful of you," Simon goes.

"I know," I say. It wasn't a bad touch. It was just a friendly touch. That's all it was.

"Not back there with Dawn, or just now, either."

"I know," I say. The heat's coming up off the road in ripply waves, and a part of me wants to ask Simon what makes it do that, exactly, but the other part of me doesn't let my mouth open.

"Well, all right, then," Simon says into the messy air.

"Did you tell him?" Tim goes as soon as Simon disappears into the bathroom.

"Tell him what?" Stacy asks. Everybody's crowding around, grabbing their drinks and McNuggets and things before I even have a chance to take it all out of the bags.

"Nothing," Tim says.

"Did he do anything?" Stacy goes, and everybody gets quiet. Stacy presses closer. "Did he?"

I don't know. It was just a don't-worry-about-it touch. A friendly touch. That's all it was.

"Alex!" Stacy eyes are kind of bloodshot. "What did he do?"

"Nothing," I say, looking at Tim for some reason. "He just touched my leg." Why did I say that? Tim's mouth opens, and the others kind of breathe in all at once. Stacy taps my thigh with her good hand.

"There?" she asks. "Did he touch you there?"

How did she know?

"I knew it!" Stacy goes. "I told you so!" She flicks her hair. "I bet you liked it," she says. "You did, didn't you, you perv!"

"I did not!" I yell. "*I'm* not the pervert!"

Tim's face crumples, like a photograph swallowed by flame, and he bolts toward the double doors.

I chase him all the way to the stream, where he squats, hunched up on the bank.

"I didn't mean it like it sounded," I say. It's so hot.

"It doesn't matter," Tim tells me. "He touched you!" His face is red, like the way Teddy's gets all the time, and there's a shine on his upper lip.

"It wasn't like Stacy made it seem." Was it? "It wasn't like what Simon did to her."

"See?" Tim says. "Now you believe he did something to her."

"No, I don't," I argue, but I can hear how I sound. Uncertain.

"You just said you did."

The truth is, I don't know anymore. I'm confused.

"Maybe some of it's my fault," I say low. "Maybe I shouldn't have said I wanted to go with him alone."

Maybe if I hadn't seen his thing, or if I had yelled when I did . . . If I hadn't gotten that feeling, that melting and sliding, that time he touched my chest. Maybe he knew about that somehow and then knew about it again when it happened today. Maybe he saw me watching him and Dawn, just standing there watching. Did I make him think the wrong thing?

"I hate him!" Tim says, and then he spits into the stream.

No. It was just a friendly touch. Just a nothing touch. I grab Tim by the shoulders and shake him once, so hard, his head snaps back and forth like a rag doll's.

"You do not hate him!" I say.

He reaches up to pry my fingers away. I can't help it. I creep my hands back to where they were. I make him look at me.

"We don't hate him," I say.

17

I CALL TIM from my rocker in my bedroom. It's late.

"I can't sleep," I say.

"Yeah," his voice cracks over the phone. "I know what you mean."

My dad knew something was really wrong when he got home from work. I don't know how he knew, but he tried to get me to talk about it. And then when my mom came home way later, she tried. Only I couldn't. I wanted to, but I didn't know how. What was I going to say, anyway? *Simon's been . . . Simon is . . .* Been what? Is what? No way.

"You want to come over tomorrow after school?" I ask Tim now.

"Okay." We're quiet a second.

"Bring your ball," I go. "Mine's flat, and I broke the needle on my pump."

"Okay," he says.

"So in the fall we'll really be a team," I go. "Officially and everything."

"Yeah," he says. He doesn't sound too psyched. "And Simon will be our coach. Officially."

We sound careful. Like if we speak too loud, we might break something.

"I don't feel too good," I say.

"I don't either," Tim says.

We hang up pretty soon after that.

When I walk through the double doors from the driveway into the lower school, Maggie's there with a man and a woman I've never seen before.

Maggie waggles her index finger. "Morning, Alex," she goes. "This is Mr. and Mrs. Prescott."

"Hi." I nod as polite as I can.

"Nice to meet you," the man says.

"The Prescotts have a daughter about your age," Maggie says. "They're thinking of sending her here next year."

"She goes to Lincoln now," Mrs. Prescott tells me.

"Lincoln sucks," I say, before I know what I'm doing.

"Alex!" Maggie goes.

"It certainly does," Mr. Prescott agrees, and Maggie lets me go.

At the slate path practically everyone's outside, except for Stacy. It's too hot to be outside.

Tim rolls the soccer ball over to me, and I knock it back.

"Why's everybody out here?" I ask Viv. I know why, but I have to ask anyway, while I try to think of what to do. Viv stares straight at me from underneath his turban, but he doesn't say anything. "Come on," I say.

"Nobody wants to be near Simon."

"That's stupid!"

Viv nods. "Maybe."

"It wasn't like Stacy made it seem," I tell all of them. I try to sound as sure as I can.

Simon opens the upper school doors and yells out to us. "Let's go!" We gather up our things and trickle inside. Simon crosses his arms and leans back on the heels of his feet. "You're all late." Nobody says anything. "Want to tell me what's going on?" Simon's looking at me and Tim. His eyebrows are all pulled together, thick and worried.

"Beats me," Tim mumbles. I shrug.

The day gets worse and worse. Nobody wants to do any

work with Simon, and he can't figure out what's happening. His glass room is empty, and everybody's being really quiet, like it's a silent study day, only it's not. The Prescotts visit for about fifteen minutes to double-check that they want to send their daughter here.

"Are they always this focused?" Mr. Prescott asks, and Simon runs his hands through his hair.

"No," he says. "Something's wrong." The Prescotts laugh at that, even though Simon didn't mean it as a joke.

After they leave, Simon stands in front of the science counter and claps his hands together twice. Then he asks us all, straight out, "You going to let me in on this thing?" Nobody says a word. "Tim?" Tim shakes his head. "Alex?"

"It's just a misunderstanding," I say. That's what it is.

"Is that right?"

"Yeah," I say. That's really what it is.

"Is Stacy involved in this misunderstanding?"

"Yeah."

"Anybody know where she is today?" Simon looks around the room again. But nobody knows. Simon waits it out for a while, staring at each one of us, making us squirm. We don't say anything, though, and finally he gives up.

"All right." He sighs. "Eat your lunch."

* * *

Today's the first day we can use our new field, and we eat fast. There's not much talking on our run through the playground. It's still way more hot than usual this time of year, and we're kind of out of it. We pick teams quick, though, and start playing. The fresh grass improves our game somehow. The ball moves smoother, or straighter maybe. I'm glad for the way my body takes over, letting my mind go blank. Glad for the chance to do nothing but follow the ball and shouts until the ugliness of the past days drifts away, leaving the green of the ground mixed with the black and white and red flash of our cleats. I don't think about anything. I don't worry about anything. I just run and breathe. Kick, dribble, and dodge.

Sebastian interrupts our game, stumbling into a fall onto our new grass, landing on his side.

"Maggie wants you, Alex," he goes. "Right now." Then, before I can even register that much, he says, "And your parents are here."

The first thing I see in the lower school building is Stacy's father stalking out the double doors, stiff and tall, like a living statue. The next thing I see is Maggie and Simon, both of them huddled by the painted mural, his hands bunching in and out of fists at his sides. Then my parents are there—why aren't they at work?—rushing me into Maggie's office. I can hear Maggie's and Simon's voices hissing and low, all the way across the lobby.

". . . next to them at the tent . . . ," Maggie's saying. Simon argues something back at her, and then Maggie cuts him off. ". . . I've always said that about rappelling, and you . . ." My father clears his throat, trying to cover up their talk. It works a little, but not much. ". . . that ladder for years . . . you were thinking?"

"What's going on?" I ask. "What are you doing here?" Maggie pokes her head in the doorway.

"We haven't had a chance to talk to her," my mother says.

"The detective will be here any minute," Maggie goes, and then she closes the door on her way back to Simon.

My mom sinks into one of two chairs and pats the other one for me to sit in. I do, and my dad squats a little on the floor, sort of between us.

"What is it?" I ask again, loud this time.

"Stacy's arm is infected," my mom starts.

"Is she going to die?" That's the only thing I can think of that might have brought my parents and Stacy's father here. The detective part, I don't get.

"No, she's going to be fine," my mom answers. "But it seems she hadn't had a full medical checkup in a long time.

Not even when she was in the hospital for her broken arm." She stops and looks at my dad.

"Mom!" My stomach is clenching and unclenching like Simon does with his fists. My mother opens her mouth to keep going, but then she closes it again. My dad puts his hand on her shoulder, his arm resting across my neck to reach her. Now I'm really scared. "Tell me!"

My father takes over. "The doctor who examined Stacy this time didn't just look at her arm. He did a complete workup, and it seems he had some questions after that, and Stacy told him that Simon—" Now he stops. All this stopping and starting is making me crazy. "That Simon has been doing things, sexual things, to her." I feel a riot in my guts.

"Stacy lies!"

"We know," my father says, but then he goes on like that doesn't matter. "She also said"—I can feel his arm tense up—"Stacy also told the doctor about Simon doing things with you, too. Also sexual things."

"But she lies!"

"We know Stacy lies sometimes, Alex," my mother says. "But you don't, and we need to know the truth."

"No matter what it is," my father goes. "It's very important."

The door opens again, and now Maggie walks in, holding some folding chairs, and there's a man behind her. He's got a mole on his nose, and he looks hot in his suit, and for a minute I think he's someone who wants to send his kid to our school.

"This is Detective Edwards," Maggie tells us. She starts unfolding the extra chairs and passing them around so everyone can sit. She does it without looking at any of us.

"Does this have to be done right away?" my mom asks. "We've had no time with her to . . . to prepare." Prepare for what?

"You can wait if you want," the detective says. "But we tend to clear these things up a little quicker when we keep it informal at first." He looks at each of us separately before he goes on. "With everyone here now, it sure would make my job easier just to go ahead and get this out of the way."

"I don't like this," my father says to Maggie, and then Simon walks in, his face a sick gray color. I wonder why Stacy's father didn't kill him yet.

We sit in a tight circle, and it's crowded. My father has a chair now, but he keeps his arm across my neck. The detective starts talking. He shakes my hand and tells me his name again and then tells me my name and age, even though I already know my own name and age. Then he reaches into the inside of his jacket and pulls out a handheld. He flips it open.

"Stacy Janice has quite a list of events she says pertain to you and your teacher." *Pertain.* That's a Teddy word. I think it means "has to do with." "Touching on the back, arm, shoulder, thigh, breast." My face goes hot. My mom adds her arm to my dad's, crossed over my shoulders, and that helps keep me from crying. "Exposure of the penis." I hold my eyes as wide as they'll go and try to breathe. I want to be playing soccer. I want to be passing to Tim and ducking around Viv and kicking the ball, far, far across the field. "Sleeping on top of you inside a tent. Hugging." My father rubs the back of my neck with his thumb. The detective makes a mark with his stylus, and I think I'll die if there's more. "Stacy Janice also says she told you of an incident during which your teacher molested her while she was in the principal's office, injured."

"That's this office," I say, thinking how horrible the word *molested* sounds. That's something real perverts do. The detective looks around the room and then scribbles another note.

"I see, Alex." He talks while he's writing. "Then you can verify that event?" My father's thumb stops moving.

"No!" I glance over at Simon. He's sitting straighter

than I've ever seen him. "I mean, Stacy told me it happened. But—" The detective cuts me off.

"What exactly did she tell you?"

"She just said he did stuff to her when she broke her arm and was in here bleeding and everything."

"That's ridiculous!" Simon bursts out. He never interrupts. He looks at Maggie, but she doesn't look back at him. The detective makes another note. "Ann," Simon goes. "Jack."

"If you'd like to do this more formally, sir, you're welcome to leave this interview and get yourself a lawyer," the detective says.

"I don't need a lawyer!" Simon goes. "Tell them, Alex!"

The detective leans forward and puts his forearms on his knees. "If you can just tell us which parts you know for a fact happened and which ones you know for a fact didn't," the detective says to me, "that's all we need."

Simon lets out a big breath, like he's relieved to hear that, and I think about what I know for a fact and what I don't. It's hard because I keep feeling his fingers brushing my chest, and I keep seeing his thing, thick and slippery in the night rain, and his mouth on Dawn's, and then his hand on my thigh. It's so hard because I only know what happened, but not what it means. And this might be the most important time ever in my whole life to be fair. To be a decent human being. For Stacy and for Simon. Otherwise, my parents wouldn't be here, and Simon's face wouldn't be gray, and they wouldn't all be looking at me like it mattered more than anything ever mattered before. And to be fair, I'm supposed to tell the truth. And telling the truth means telling the facts.

"Simon's touched me sometimes," I start, and I feel my mother's hand tighten around my father's. Simon's chair creaks as he shifts in it. The detective holds his arm out in front of Simon, like a seat belt, and I rush to finish because I'm scared. "Not in the way Stacy makes it seem," I say. But then I have to tell it all. "I mean, nothing he did ever seemed like it was wrong until Stacy started talking."

"And then what?" the detective asks.

"I don't know." I'm trying to think, but the detective isn't giving me time.

"Did you see this man's penis?" he asks me.

"Yes. But . . . he was . . . he was just using the bathroom." That was an accident. I know that was just an accident.

"There was a bathroom on a camping trip?" The detective sounds mad now.

"We were near these latrine pits, where we were all supposed to go, and it was raining and dark, and it was just an accident I saw anything!" I say, but it sounds strange now, out loud. It doesn't sound right.

"What about the touching?" the detective asks, flipping his handheld closed, like he doesn't even need it anymore. "In a tent and, I believe, at other times. At school." He looks at Simon, even though he's talking to me. "Yesterday. In a car?"

"I told you," I try again. "He's touched me sometimes. But it was accidents or just—just . . ." I don't know how to describe it. Simon's shaking his head, his face the color of cinder blocks.

"Alex," my father reminds me, "take your time." But there is no time because they're all staring at me, waiting for an answer. Waiting for me to tell them something I don't know. What?

"I don't know," I say. "I don't know."

18

WHEN THE DETECTIVE asks if Simon ever tried to touch me with his penis, my mother doesn't give me a second to answer.

"Enough!" she says. "That's enough!" She stands, yanking me up with her. "If you find it necessary to question my child further," she tells the detective, "you'll have to arrange a *formal* interview."

The detective slowly tucks the handheld back into his jacket. "It's up to you," he says as my dad stands up next to me and my mother. "But these things can get tricky." Simon stays in his seat, staring straight ahead, his eyes fixed on a blown-glass paperweight holding down Maggie's desk. "Legally speaking, that is. Not to mention that I'm sure you'll want to find out what—" My mother interrupts him.

"We'll finish this ourselves," she snaps, putting her hand on the small of my back and pushing me toward the door. "In the privacy of our own home."

"We'll get to the bottom of this," my dad whispers to Simon, as we walk out of there. I don't say anything, because Simon's new cinder-block face scares the voice out of me and because I don't know what's okay to say anymore.

Nobody talks all the way home, and then, when we're getting out of the car, my mother goes, "*Did* Simon ever do that?"

"Do what?" I ask.

"Try to touch you with his penis?"

"No!"

"Are you sure?" Our voices echo here in the garage, and I lower mine because I don't like this stuff bouncing around back and forth.

"I'm positive," I say, glad to be sure of at least one thing.

Upstairs, neither of my parents stretch out on their bed like they usually do. Instead, my mother picks up her hairbrush from the bureau and starts pulling silver strands out in clumps. She just stands there, pulling. My father paces. He goes from one side of the bed to the other. Back and forth. I sit cross-legged right in the center of the mattress.

My mom pulls and pulls at her brush. "Alex," she goes, "deep down . . . deep down inside of you—"

"Ann, don't," my father says, and he stops pacing. The mirror on the wall behind him reflects the wrinkles in the back of his blue shirt.

"Deep down," my mother goes, like she hasn't even heard my dad speak, "don't you know what the truth is?" I can't guess what she's thinking. Does she believe Simon really is a pervert? Or is she mad because she thinks he isn't and I said he touched me? "Alex?" my mom goes.

"The detective said I should tell the facts," I say. "And I did." I look at my dad, hoping he'll ask her to stop again or maybe tell me what they believe the truth is. But now he's quiet. Waiting.

"What is it you feel?" he asks. "What does your gut tell you about Simon?"

My gut. Well, it's angry at him for not being more careful at the latrine pits and for coming into our tent to sleep. And my gut feels sorry for him for the way all the kids stopped talking to him and for how his face looked today in Maggie's office. And it's confused by him because of the way he turned into a man when he used to be just my teacher. And I guess it loves him because he's Simon. And when I think about that, think about who he is and how he's always been with me, with all of us, I'm not confused anymore.

"He's not like that," I tell them finally. "I know he's not like that." They know what I mean by *that*. My father takes a deep breath and lets it out really slow, and my mother drops the hairbrush onto the bed.

"Why didn't you just say so to the detective?" she goes. Her voice is soft, but her words feel like claws.

"I was trying to tell the facts." I can feel the weight of it in my throat. Don't they know? "Everybody said I had to tell the exact truth."

"But, Alex," my mom says, "the truth isn't always only what the facts are. A lot of times it's also what you feel."

And suddenly I'm so mad at them, at all of them. "I tried to tell you how I felt a long time ago!" It rises up inside of me like a tornado, twisting and bucking to leap out. "I tried and tried, and you wouldn't listen! You just kept interrupting or going off on your big emergencies or saying how I should be fair! How I should be her stupid friend!" And I'm off the bed, down the stairs, and out the front door.

I run hard and fast toward Tim's house. But I'm not even halfway there when it hits me what's happened, what's really happened, and my lungs hitch and my back kicks, and I stumble to my knees because it hurts so much to breathe.

My father finds me bent over myself in the street, coughing and crying. "I ruined it," I choke. "They'll send him to jail!"

"Alex," my dad whispers, leaning over me. "We'll fix it."

I'm so stupid, I want to say. *How could I have been so stupid?* But I'm shaking all over, shaking so hard with what I've done to Simon that my teeth are clicking, and I can't speak. My father lifts me up, like I'm a baby, and I curl my legs around his waist and wrap my arms around his neck, and he carries me home.

Tim, Sophie, and I are sitting at the trapezoid table the next morning. The other kids want to know what's going on, but other than swearing that Simon never did anything wrong, not once, my mouth is sealed shut. Simon's not here, and it's five minutes past flash card time. Stacy's not here either.

"There's no proof," Sophie whispers to Tim and me. She's been cool about not telling the other kids anything either. "I heard my mom talking. Alex, the detective believes what your parents told him over the phone last night. And Stacy has no proof."

"Where's Simon, then?" Tim asks. Sophie shakes her head.

"What's going on?" Sebastian asks for the millionth time. "I just want to know what's going on!"

Maggie walks in with some woman wearing huge hoop earrings and round glasses.

"This is Sheryl," Maggie announces. "She's going to be substituting for us. Please make her feel at home."

"Maggie?" Tim goes.

"Yes."

"Is Simon coming back?"

Maggie looks down at her wedged heels and then back at us again. "I don't have the answer to that." What does she mean?

"Maggie?"

"Yes, Marie?"

"Where's Stacy?"

It's a good question. I wonder what Stacy's doing right now. I wonder if she's thinking up more lies. If her arm hurts or if her father's smashed anything else at their house.

"I'm not . . . ," Maggie begins, but then she changes her mind. "Stacy's arm is infected, and she's staying home for a few days."

Maybe Stacy's talking to that detective right now. Maybe she's got her hand on her hip, and she's making him feel like an idiot.

Maggie leaves our classroom, and Sheryl picks me. "You're Alex," she says. How does she know? "Maybe you could show me around a little. Let me know how things work here." I drag myself out of my chair.

"Everybody has a contract," I say as I walk her into the silent study room. My voice sounds strange, like I'm a windup toy with the battery running out. Sheryl nods.

"Maggie mentioned those," she says.

"Simon keeps his copy in there." I point to his top right desk drawer. "And we each keep a copy in our locker." That sounds funny to me. *Copy in our locker. Copy in our locker. Clapper. Clock her.* I giggle. Sheryl looks confused.

"What's so funny?" she asks. Her hoops sway from her earlobes. I stop laughing just as fast as I started. Sheryl touches the wire bridge of her glasses. She doesn't push them up or anything. She just touches the wire.

"Sorry," I say. "Maybe you better ask somebody else to help you." I leave her in the silent study room and walk right out of the upper school.

"Where are you going?" Tim shouts after me, but I don't even slow down.

I walk through all the double doors and head for Maple Avenue. Nobody stops me. I keep going, turning off at the road my mother took when she drove me to Stacy's that time. The heat still hasn't let up, and water beads on my chest, in between my stupid starter boobs.

I walk and I sweat. The trees lining Stacy's neighborhood are huge, their leaves weaving a canopy over the streets. Magic Marker red-and-yellow tulips lift their faces toward the driveways and sidewalks, like little guards, keeping colorful watch. It's cooler here, but the air still hangs over itself, invisible and thick.

I make a right at Park Place and shove my hands deep into my shorts pockets when I see Stacy's house. There's a U-Haul truck parked in her driveway.

"What are you doing here?" Stacy says, running to the screen door to meet me. She's glancing over her shoulder like she's nervous about something. Her arm has a fresh cast on it, white this time. The circles under her eyes are laced through with tiny blue veins. In another room somewhere behind Stacy, I see two men carrying a couch, and next to them her mom is holding its cushions.

"Who are they?" I go.

"Neighbors."

"Are you moving?" What a strange time to be moving.

"You better leave," she says.

"No."

Stacy looks over her shoulder again, dips her head toward her chest for a second, and then looks out at me through the haze of mesh screen. I catch glimpses of neighbor movers carrying lamps and stacks of books—sometimes a box that hasn't even been taped up.

"You're going to get me in trouble," she goes, slipping through the door and pulling me down her steps to the side yard.

"So?" I say. "You got me and Simon in trouble."

"Why did you come here?" she asks.

"I want you to tell the truth."

She pokes a tail of hair into her mouth and chews it for a while. "I can't tell you the truth," she says.

"Why?"

"I just can't."

"Simon never touched you, did he?" She won't answer. I know he didn't because I can feel it. I felt it the whole time, really, but she confused me. "Did he!" I ask again. I need her to be honest. Just once. She shakes her head a tiny, tiny bit. There.

We listen to the voices and thumps, the calls and bangs coming from the house and truck. I hear a phone ring. It rings and rings and rings.

"Why don't you just go?" Stacy says.

"Why are you moving?" I say back.

"My father doesn't like it here anymore."

"That's not fair," I tell her. Stacy snorts. "Can't he wait until the school year is over?" It doesn't make sense. Stacy shakes her head. Not such a tiny shake this time. "I wish you hadn't lied," I say.

"Nobody believes the truth anyway," she says. I don't understand why she thinks that. She can tell I don't understand. I know by the way she groans and rolls her eyes at me. "Look. I'm sorry," she goes. "Tell Simon I'm sorry, okay?"

"What about Tim?" I say. "And everybody else?" She ignores that.

Instead, she whispers, "Alex—"

"Stacy!" I hear her father yell. She jumps.

"Stacy!" I know he must be inside the house somewhere, but his voice is so loud, he could be right next to us.

"Alex," she says, still in a whisper, but fast, "I have to tell you something."

"Stacy!" He's nearer now, maybe by the open front door, just behind the screen. She turns toward it and then turns back to me.

"What?" I ask, but I already know that whatever it is, I'm not going to believe her. She tosses her hair. It shines under the sun. "What!" I say.

Stacy flicks her eyes toward the house again and goes still. She doesn't move for the longest moment. Doesn't blink, doesn't even breathe. Then she makes a noise in her throat, a scratching noise I've never heard before, and she lifts her chin, like she's just thought of something, and she looks me straight in the eyes.

"You're the nicest person I've ever known," she says. And she's gone, loping toward the front door, her cast bright and clunking at her side, skinny legs quick and sharp, carrying her forward and away.

A police car slows to a stop next to me. I'm sitting under some trees. Just sitting. I've been here for a bunch of hours. Practically the whole day, I think. "Aren't you supposed to be in school?" the cop yells through the window.

"Yeah," I yell back. He drives me, and Maggie's lips are pressed tight when we show up at her office door inside the lower school.

"That's a nice wall," the officer tells her, pointing to our mural on his way out.

"Thank you," she says. When he's gone, Maggie clamps her hand on my shoulder. "I thought you were down by the stream all this time," she says. "I had no idea you left the premises." I wait. "Where did you go?"

"To see Stacy."

"You went to her house?"

I nod. "They're moving," I say.

"What do you mean, they're moving?"

"There was a truck there this morning, and they were loading furniture into it, and Stacy said her dad thinks it's time to go." Maggie loosens her grip on me.

"You may be excused," she tells me, her hand snaking toward the phone. "I expect you to return to class."

But I don't. I walk up to the soccer field. I walk right to the center and lie on my back. It's still hotter than anything, but I don't care. I close my eyes and try to figure out what it means if I'm the nicest person Stacy's ever known. Because I never really thought about it before, but now that I am thinking, I don't see how it could be close to true.

So maybe Stacy hasn't known such great people.

Which confuses me even more. Especially because, even though her lies were the sickest ones I've ever heard, even though she pulled my hair that time, Stacy was nice, underneath all that. I remember the way she taught Teddy three-card monte. When she gave the good marshmallow stick to Marie, and how she grabbed my hand that morning when I thought Tim might die during his oral report.

I want to know why she lied.

My dad picks up the phone on the first ring, right as he and my mom walk in the door from work. It's Maggie, but I guess she forgets to tell on me for skipping almost a whole day of school because while my dad listens to her, he doesn't even glance my way.

"Alex, please leave us alone," he says after he hangs up.

"What is it?" my mom asks him, and I don't move. He digs the heels of his palms into his eyes.

"Alex," he goes.

"I'm not leaving," I tell him. "I want to know what's going on."

He waits a second, and then he looks at my mother. "There are no charges against Simon," he tells her. "Apparently, Stacy's family has moved. Their house is empty. Nobody seems to know where they've gone." He crosses the kitchen and puts his arms around her. "I knew it," I hear him whisper. My mom hugs him, and over his shoulder, I see her squeezing her face closed. "I knew it," he whispers again, like he's done something wrong.

"What?" I say. My mother reaches to pull me into their hug. But I won't budge, so they step apart. My father keeps his back to me.

"We think it's Stacy's father; not Simon," he finally says, in this clogged voice.

"Stacy's father what?" I ask, even though a little piece of me, somewhere deep in my brain, knows exactly what he's trying to say. My dad won't turn around.

"We think it's Stacy's father who did those things to her," my mom starts to explain, and then her words trail off as she dips her silvery head toward the floor.

I don't want to understand. I don't want to know what they mean, but the thing is, I do. It's so hard to think about it that my mind and my blood sort of stop for a while, and it's like I'm up above somewhere, watching the three of us standing here in the kitchen, together and apart, silent and still.

19

ON MONDAY MORNING the double doors are propped open. The heat wave broke over the weekend, finally, and now it's perfect cool spring weather. Sheryl's at the front of the room with Simon's flash cards. *Loco, trans, cart.* She's going way too fast.

"Slow down!" Sebastian goes. "Lady, you've got to slow down!" A couple of kids titter at that, and Sebastian offers to hold up the cards himself, and then more people titter, and then Simon walks in. He moves fast, right up to the science counter.

My heart and my stomach kick right at the same time. It's okay. Simon's back, and he's okay. Tim shoves at my knee. He's grinning. He hasn't smiled for days. But the others look worried. That's because they still don't know what to think, even though I've told them over and over what the truth is about Simon. The real truth. Not just the facts.

Simon whispers something to Sheryl, and she nods and moves over a little to give him room. We wait for her to say *Good-bye* or *Good luck* or something, but she doesn't. We wait for her to wave and pick up her pocketbook on her way out, but she doesn't. She's not leaving. Marie, of all people, figures it out first.

"Why's she staying?" she asks. Sheryl touches her glasses.

"Sheryl is staying because I'm not," Simon goes.

"Are you sick?" That's Teddy.

"No." Simon bunches his lips together and looks over at me and Tim. "Not sick." He doesn't loop one ankle around the other, like usual. He stands stiff, hands behind his back. "Just can't stay."

"You mean, today," Viv says, really steady, like a statement. Not a question.

"No. I mean for the rest of the year," Simon says. "The year after that, too." It's so quiet, we can hear the faucet dripping from the kitchen.

"Why?" Tim asks. He's sitting straight in his chair, as straight as Simon's standing. Simon stares down the center of the room. Sheryl excuses herself, quiet, to the side hallway. We hear the bathroom door open and then close.

"It's no secret there's been some unpleasant talk spreading around this classroom," Simon goes. "About me."

"But none of it's true," I call out. To fix it, to make right what's gone wrong.

"Nice to hear you say that, Alex," Simon says.

He's mad. He's mad at me for not saying what I should have in Maggie's office. Heads turn my way. They don't know. They don't understand. "The way I see it," Simon goes on, "a lot of . . . unfortunate things have happened lately. And I made some poor choices that didn't help matters." Now he glances around the room at us and runs his hands through his hair. "It's hard for you to learn when you're not sure about the person teaching you, and I think some of you aren't too sure about me anymore." Simon sort of nods at all of us. "I guess it's . . . hard for me, too. Hard enough that I have to leave." He takes a breath. "I just wanted to say I'm sorry if anybody in this room feels I hurt you in any way. I sure didn't mean to." He looks right at Tim. "And I wanted to say good-bye." His feet stay planted flat on the floor. We look at him. We don't look at him. Nobody knows what to do. I don't know what to do. "All right, then," Simon says, and he leaves through the open double doors.

Tim shoves his chair back, knocking it to the ground.

He races after Simon, and we can all see and hear them out there.

"You can't leave!" Tim shouts. Simon keeps going, following the cheerful pansy-lined slate toward the lower school. "You can't leave!" Tim screams again, grabbing a small stone from the ground and hurling it just when Simon reaches the end of the path. The stone hits Simon square in the back. He stops walking. Tim stays where he is. Simon turns around.

"Timothy," Simon says. Then he leans backward against the lower school doors. In a second he's gone.

20

THE NEXT DAY we don't do any work at all. Maggie meets with us at flash card time to try to explain things.

"Simon's going to take a job at a school in another county," she says.

"Why can't he come back here?" Teddy asks.

"He can," Maggie tells us. "And I wish he would. But he's made another choice." She passes out Simon's new work address.

"No e-mail?" Sebastian goes.

"He didn't leave me an e-mail address," Maggie says. "But he hopes you'll write snail mail to him anytime you want about anything at all. He made me promise to let you know that he'll write back."

"This is all Stacy's fault," Danny says while I watch

Tim fold Simon's address carefully and slip it into his back pocket.

"We're having a workshop today," Maggie goes. "In about half an hour a few guest speakers are going to join Sheryl and me, and we're going to talk together about what's happened and how everybody's feeling." Danny rolls his eyes, just like Stacy used to do.

"Stacy lied about Simon being a pervert, and then she disappeared, and then Simon left because we all made him feel so bad, and now we feel crappy about it," he goes. "What's there to talk about?"

"Not *crappy*," Maggie says. "*Badly* or *guilty* or *sad* are more descriptive and accurate words." She waits a second to make sure we get her point. Who cares. "We need to talk about what it's like when somebody leaves us unexpectedly. And we need to discuss this 'pervert' issue. It's important to understand what that really means."

We spend the morning talking about Stacy and Simon, and some of the reasons why they might have left, and whether we'll see them again, and how we feel, and how they might feel.

The other kids think Stacy disappeared because her family was embarrassed that she lied. But Tim and Sophie and I know it's more than that. Stacy left because her dad made her. Because he's the one who's the pervert, and if the police find him, he'll be in a lot of trouble. Tim and Sophie and I know that, but we don't say it because Maggie doesn't and because it's way too horrible.

In the afternoon Maggie and the guest speakers switch to talking about sexual abuse. About how nobody is allowed to touch you anyplace that a small bathing suit would cover unless you're grown and you want them to. About how nobody is allowed to have you touch them either, in those places, until you're grown and you both want to. About how an adult is never supposed to touch a kid anywhere in a way that's different from a regular hug or a regular kiss, different from regular roughhousing. About how adults aren't allowed to do that different kind of touching, even if the kid thinks it might feel good, because adults know the rules and aren't allowed to get confused the way kids are allowed to.

They talk about how you have the right to say no, to tell somebody to stop. How you should never make it up if it really never happened. They teach us how you should always tell someone you trust if bad touching happened to you, even and especially if the bad touching is from somebody you care about, because that person needs help to stop doing it. How it's never, ever your own fault.

We spend the whole afternoon in little groups and in big groups, inventing skits about it, raising our hands to ask the easier questions and writing down the hard ones on pale blue Post-its. Our guest speakers use words like *penis*, *vagina*, *breast*, *bottom*, *assertiveness*, *discomfort*, and *courage*. We listen and talk with red faces and tight voices, our eyes on the ceiling and floor. Maggie and Sheryl and the guest speakers try to make it okay, try to make it seem normal to use those words and talk about those things. But on top of how not normal it is, all I can think of is how it's too late. For Stacy. For Simon. It's too late.

At dinner I hand over the letter to parents that Maggie asked us to bring home. It has Simon's address and explains that we're going to have more workshops each week until the end of school, which isn't too far away now at all. The letter lists the names of all the guest speakers. It invites the parents to join an after-school workshop just for adults next week.

"How did it go today?" my father asks, after he reads it. He pokes at his food with a fork. We haven't eaten very much. Baked potatoes and greasy chunks of broiled chicken are hardening on our plates.

"I don't know," I say.

"Do you have any questions for me or Mom?"

"Uh-uh," I lie.

My mother pushes aside her plate and puts her elbows on the table. "Alex," she says, "you might not want to discuss things now. But later, maybe next week, maybe in a month, you might want to talk." Her eyes dart over to my dad.

He's nodding. "You can come to us anytime." For some reason, I feel tears fill up my eyes.

Why didn't Stacy's mother help her? I want to ask. *How could her father treat Stacy like that?* But somehow, by now, I know it's pointless. *Will Simon ever forgive us?* Those questions are the kind that don't have any good answers. And the thing is, even though my parents are doctors, and even though they're decent human beings, they didn't really know how to help. So I shake my head and blink my eyes and keep quiet.

"You'll write to Simon," my father says after a while. He's not asking.

"I don't know what to write."

"We'll help you," my dad says.

"I can't," I argue.

"You have to." They say it loud, both at the same time.

A few days later, after Tim gets his hair cut, we go to see *E.T.* They're showing it in a movie theater, so kids can see it on a big screen, like the way it was when it first came out. When we get to the ticket window, I step out of line.

"What's the matter?" Tim says. They chopped off all his curls. It makes him look older, tougher.

"Let's not pay," I go.

"What?"

"Just to see if we can get away with it." He doesn't like that idea. So we sort of silently compromise. He gets back in line to buy his ticket while I wait. Then we walk to the man in the bow tie who tears the stubs before letting you in. Tim hands over his ticket, and I look at him.

"Don't you have mine?" I go. I flash my dimple. "Shoot." I check my pockets. "I just had it a few minutes ago." The bow tie man looks aggravated. "Do I have to buy another one?" I make my eyes go wide. He lets me in. Easy as pie.

"I can't believe you did that," Tim goes.

"I'll pay them back on the way out," I promise.

The movie's good. We both cry in the middle, when we think E.T. dies, and then again, when he has to leave Earth and go home. At first I feel stupid for crying, and then I feel stupid that Tim's crying too. But when nobody in the whole audience gets up after the movie's over, and you can hear people sniffing and blowing their noses, I don't feel so dumb. I put my head on Tim's shoulder, the way I used to do with Simon, and he rests his head on top of mine. It feels good.

"Don't tell anyone I cried," Tim says when we finally stand up.

"Don't tell anyone I did," I go.

Our sneakers crunch and stick on popcorn and candy wrappers as we make our way down the aisle. I think we're headed for the video games, but instead, Tim leads me out to the parking lot, behind a van.

"What are you doing?" I ask. He kisses me on the cheek. Light. Then he moves away.

"Don't tell anybody," he says. I lean forward and kiss him on the mouth. Fast.

"Don't you tell anybody," I say right back. We kiss a few more times. I don't exactly feel that melting thing because I'm too nervous that I'm not kissing right. But it's pretty nice anyway.

I try to write that letter.

Dear Simon, yesterday there was this chipmunk that got into the upper school somehow, and . . .

Dear Simon, I'm really sorry that I didn't . . .

I try, but it's too hard.

* * *

That was about a month ago, and school is practically over now. Things aren't the same at all. Everybody's been sort of grumpy with everybody else, and nobody even talks about Stacy or Simon, except for the guest speakers on workshop days. Sheryl's okay, but she does things different from what we're used to. Plus, she's not Simon.

Also, Danny likes me, which makes me nervous because Marie came to school with, of all things, a blue streak in her hair, and she's been flirting with Danny, and I just like him as a friend, and I don't want anybody to get jealous of anybody else. Nobody knows Tim and I kissed that night at the movies, and we haven't done it again, and things are pretty much the same with me and him. Except our parents don't let us have sleepovers anymore. I miss having him in the next bed sometimes. I miss making tent forts and sneaking down to the kitchen with him to have cold chicken legs and Oreos in the middle of the night.

"It's not like we're going to have sex or anything!" I yelled at my parents after they made Tim go home one night after dinner.

"Alex!" my mom screeched.

"We're not perverts!" I screeched back at her, and then, of all things, she laughed at me, and I ran up to my room and slammed my door so hard, the clock fell off the wall.

One kind of cool change is that Viv's got us organized so we do our own drills and stuff for the first half of recess, and we scrimmage for the second half. We want to be ready for next year, even if we don't have a coach yet. Simon would be proud of us. But I don't think anybody's written to him yet, including me and Tim, which I don't understand, really, and which leaves this pain somewhere inside that flashes up from my stomach into my throat. It's not the same kind of pain as when Danny smashed into me on the soccer field a few years ago. It's worse.

Walking home from school with Tim our last week, I decide to bring up Simon.

"Maybe he'll change his mind and come back next year, at least to coach," I say. We stop on the path in the woods. Some crows start complaining at us from the treetops.

"I don't care," Tim answers.

"Liar."

"It doesn't matter anyway," Tim says. "I'm not coming back next year."

"What?"

He kicks at a pile of rotting twigs with his sneaker. "My parents said it's about time I go to a real school, and my grandmother's going to help pay to send me to St. John's."

"St. John's!" The crows fly off, their wings sounding like

sheets being snapped in the wind. "But next year's our last year!"

"I hate Forest Alternative now," Tim goes. He starts walking again. I follow. "Don't you?" I don't want to admit it, but I do.

"It's not the same without Simon," I say instead. "I miss him." Tim spits on the ground. His spit hits a beetle. "Don't you miss him, Tim?"

I'm worried that maybe he doesn't. But he nods. Then he snaps a branch off a tree and throws it out into the brush. We can hear it clacking and crinkling through the leaves.

"Still," I say, "you can't go to St. John's."

"I know," he goes. "But they're making me." I speed up and pass him. Then I have to hold a prickly stem to the side so he won't get whipped in the face behind me.

"But then I'll be stuck all by myself," I tell him, imagining how awful it will be with Sebastian complaining about every little thing. And Marie pissed about Danny. "You can't leave!"

He pulls me to a stop, tugging at my waist and turning me around to face him. "Don't be mad," he goes. "We'll still hang out." He's holding on to my waist. His hands are warm.

"They hate girls," I remind him. "Their team wouldn't even cover me."

"I'll cover you," he says, and then he starts to smile. I don't get what's so funny. I feel miserable. "Hey." He touches my face where that rope got me and runs his finger down where the cut used to be. "It's all healed," he goes. Then he pulls me close. We haven't really hugged before, even that night after the movies. He holds me pretty tight, and this time I get that sliding feeling, all over. I don't want it to end, so when he starts pulling away, I won't let him, and then he starts to laugh, and then he stops.

21

DEAR SIMON, I hope you know how bad I feel that everything got so . . .

Dear Simon, Sheryl is really not that smart or good of a teacher, and everybody really misses you.

Dear Simon, Teddy was telling us about Zeno's paradox, only . . .

My parents went to bed a long time ago, right after they tried to help me figure out why it's so hard for me to think of what to write. My dad said I had to come up with a letter, and soon. That it's not fair, me taking so long. But I couldn't get anywhere, and now my mind is spinning, and nothing is making it quiet down. I've tried counting sheep, I've tried remembering every play of the St. John's scrimmage. I've tried deep breathing. But my brain won't shut up.

Even after I grab a flashlight from our garage, I don't know where I'm going, exactly. It's strange this late at night. Maple Avenue is empty, and everything is really quiet, except for the crickets humming like some huge refrigerator in the distance. I get to school, and I think I'm going to the soccer field, but instead, I wind up at the playground swings, dangling my feet into the little trench underneath the seat and holding on to cool, pinching chains at my sides.

I try to imagine where Simon is right now. Riding his bike through black streets? Or up in the mountains somewhere, sitting at a fire? Maybe he's with Dawn.

I arch backward, dropping my head and pumping my legs, making the swing set squeak with my moving weight. I pump a little more, a little faster, until I'm sweeping through the air in a smooth back-and-forth arc. The night rushes around my ears and insects flick at my face, and the metal links nip at my fingers as I push myself higher and higher.

"Hey, Stacy," I say right out loud. "Bet you can't do this."

And then I launch myself out of the seat, fly through the air, and land hard.

It's the end of July, and everything's been decided. I can't face going back to Forest Alternative with all that's happened and Simon and Tim not there. And my parents can't face enrolling me in any other private schools because the only other one they like is too far away, and another one is too religious, and St. John's is for boys only, and the other two have bad politics or something.

But my parents promised that if I go to Lincoln, they'll help get me on the boys' soccer team. Lincoln has a girls' team, only when we researched it, we found out that last year they always forfeited games because they never had enough players. I guess the girls at Lincoln must like some other sport better than soccer, but I don't want to be on some lame team. I want to be on a good one.

"You have to be skilled enough if we're going to push for you to play with the boys," my father had said. "It wouldn't be right if you're not up to their level and we make a fuss because you're a girl and our fuss is the only reason you make the team."

"It's going to be hard, Alex," my mother had said. "They may not like it. They might really not like it."

So now I have to pick up some stuff I left in my locker: a couple of book report poems I had to do at the end of the year for Sheryl, my calculator, a mechanical pencil, that blue sweater, and whatever else is in there. My mom keeps the car running in the parking lot, since this is supposed to be fast. We have to get to the post office before it closes, so I can send my letter to Simon, Priority Mail. My parents are making me send it that way, and they're also making me pay for it out of my allowance.

Things are overgrown between the plates of the slate path. Bees fly up out of the tall weeds when my sandals pad up to them, and the long grass makes my ankles itch. Inside the upper school the walls are bare, and the chairs and tables are shoved along the glass wall of the silent study room. The bathtub is filled with books. I don't know where all the pillows went.

My stuff is right where I left it in the locker: stray homework, a crumpled lunch bag, a comb, the blue sweater, an old pack of gum. I fish it all out, and right when I think I'm done, I knock something that rolls from one side of my locker to the other. It's a candle. The same one I gave to Stacy. The one you're supposed to light on the anniversary of someone's death. To show you remember them. To show you honor them. When I pick it up, I see how the green wax is cracked and sort of dusty. I wonder if Stacy put it in my locker the very same day she got it, and if it's been lying there, forgotten, ever since. I use my palm to wipe off the dust, and then I hold the candle close to my nose and close my eyes. It still smells just a tiny bit like pine trees. I open my eyes, trying to think if I should save the candle or not, but then I forget all about it, because in the spaces between the stacked tables and chairs, through the glass wall of the silent study room, I suddenly see Simon.

My heart flops down to my stomach and digs in, and I feel dizzy, like I've just spotted a burglar at my bedroom window or the president in the neighborhood supermarket. I hold still and try to breathe in and out. In and out.

Simon's by his desk in there, with boxes scattered every which way and piles of papers all over the place. His bike's not on the hooks or even leaned up against a glass wall. I wonder how he got here. He doesn't notice me for a second, but then, for no reason, he looks up and over and meets my eyes through the glass. Without waving or nodding or anything, he walks out.

"I left my sweater here," I say, nervous. Simon's tan, and he's wearing a pair of stiff new jeans. I look over at the boxes. Some of them are full and taped up already. "I'm not coming back either," I tell him.

"Uh-huh," Simon says, extra neutral.

"Do you know where Stacy is?" I ask him.

"How the hell would I know that?" Not neutral anymore. Just mad. His face is different than I remember. Harder or something. It scares me.

"You two left at the same time," I try to explain. A part

of me thought maybe they ended up in the same place. I guess that doesn't make much sense.

"Why didn't you tell them Stacy was a liar?"

"I did," I say. "And, anyway, I thought . . . I mean . . . You told me everybody lies."

"I told you what?"

"That everybody says stuff . . ." What was it? "You said there're things that are untrue in all the truths and things that are true in all the—" I stop because I think I'm getting it wrong and because he's looking at me like I have five heads. My teeth start to chatter, even though it's summer and I'm not cold.

"I told you nothing of the kind," he says. Spit flies out of his mouth.

"You did, too," I argue. "You said—"

He doesn't wait for me to finish. "What I said was that behind every lie there's some grain of truth! That's what I said."

"Oh." I clench my teeth to stop the chattering.

He blows air out hard through his nose and glances back at the boxes. "Do you know what this has done to me?" He sounds twisted, uneven.

"Everybody was saying I should be her friend," I tell him. "Everybody was saying I should be fair."

His jaw pushes out under his chin, and the corners of his lips start tugging. "You should have known the difference between a man who would do those things and me." Dread creeps into my skin like some kind of poison.

"I know it now," I say, ashamed.

"Everyone knows it now." His voice isn't so loud, but it's a wail anyway, thickening that dread to the inside of my bones until I think I might just die. "But we can't reverse what's been done to us, can we?"

He's right, and there's nothing I can say. Nothing that will be enough, nothing that will change how I helped mess everything up for him. He stares at me, mad and cold, just stares until I can't take it anymore, can't take what I did to him, and I grab my stuff to leave.

I'm halfway out the double doors when he says, "Wait." I turn around. He moves forward a step and then stops. He hooks one ankle around the other. I miss him so much.

"I'm sorry," he tells me. I never knew before how many different things you could be sorry over.

"So am I," I tell him back. I should have been the one to say it first. Then I remember my letter. I pull the envelope out of my back pocket. "Here." I hand it to him. "This is for you."

I slip my arms into the blue sweater, trying to think of

something else to say. But I can't, so I just take my things and walk out.

My sweater is too small. The cuffs only reach to my wrists. I peel if off and leave it on top of a chair on top of a table underneath the girl kicking a soccer ball on the wall of the lower school. Then I get into the car with my mom, who doesn't even ask what took so long.

22

IT'S THE NIGHT before school starts, and my clothes are laid out for tomorrow: new jeans; a red V-necked T-shirt, even though my mom thinks I'll be cold; my first bra, with a little yellow rose in between the cups; two sets of tiny hoops for my ears; and a seashell choker.

I'm using my heels and toes to dip and roll in my rocker while I think about this new feeling I have. It started a few weeks ago, around my thirteenth birthday, and I can tell it's important. It's this hole, this empty space I don't really get. Something I've lost and can't find because I don't know what it is, and I don't know where to look.

I've been pretty good about shoving this feeling aside when it creeps up on me, but it can be tough to shake. Then

I rewind most of last spring inside my head and play it back again, thinking maybe that's where I'll find some explanation, some answer. Obvious and easy. Like when you first look out the window of a soaring plane, and an entire city is tiny and ordered, with every piece of it in just the right place below; so small and clear, you can't believe it ever seemed complicated.

My parents drive me to Lincoln. My father packed a lunch for me, and when I peeked a second ago, there was a Hostess cupcake, a peanut-butter-and-jelly sandwich, carrot sticks, a napkin, and a piece of paper that reads *Rabbit's Foot.* My parents don't believe in real rabbit's feet, even fake real ones, because of cruelty to animals, so my dad gave me the paper instead. I guess he wants me to laugh and have good luck at the same time. The only thing is, I'm trashing the whole bag before I walk into the building. Nobody brings their own lunch to Lincoln. I know that much, at least.

"We love you," my mom says as I slam the car door. She never says that. Which makes me even more nervous than I already am.

I watch them drive away in the rush-hour traffic and feel my stomach take an elevator ride when I see all the school buses lined up in front of the building across the street. I check my watch. Five minutes till homeroom. I picture Tim at St. John's right this second, wearing a shirt and tie and scared of being beat up in the boys' room.

I have to cross Lincoln Avenue, which is a pretty busy street, in order to get to school, but I let a lot of chances go by without moving. I hear a bell ring and see kids streaming into Lincoln's different doors. Once I go in there, I'm going to start a whole new life. There's going to be new teachers and new kids and a new system, and I'm not going to know how anything works. Once I go there, I'm going to be in the ninth grade, where everybody knows everything. Where everybody is old, and the girls all have their periods already. Where Danny's cousin might hate me for wanting to be on his soccer team.

In a way, I feel a little hop of excitement. But I also feel that clump from last spring creeping up my throat. I wonder what everyone's doing in the upper school classroom. I wonder if they're scratching down flash card meanings: *Neo*: "new." *Poly*: "many." *Trans*: "across." I want to be back there, where I know how it all goes. Where it's safe.

A car zooms past me, rippling my red T-shirt. I don't know why, exactly, but right then I know I have to stop thinking that way. I can't ever go back to my old school.

Because it's different, and so am I. We've outgrown each other. I never knew you could do that with a time or a place. Only I think that's what's happened. It was such a big part of my life, but the truth is, I don't really fit into it anymore.

Another car flashes by, except when I look around, the busy traffic has slowed way down. I don't know how long I've been standing here.

There's no kids left outside. None. I'm late.

I rush across the street without even thinking, until my brain kicks in, and I'm stopped short at those double lines, trapped and in trouble. Two cars are barreling down the road in opposite directions at just the right speed and distance to tear me apart if I move forward or backward. No time to run. No time to do anything but snap my feet heel to heel, hold my breath, and throw out my arms, high and stiff like a scarecrow. I hear that loud whine of rushing air underneath blaring horns, and my shirt dances around my stomach, and the wind mangles my hair, and everything is screaming, and I wait for Simon to save me, but he doesn't, and then it's quiet except for the whoosh of one car whispering away and the other skidding to a stop, and then I'm running toward Lincoln, running from the driver, running.

* * *

My homeroom is in the green hall, number 132. There's a milky glass window set in the top third of the door, and I can see murky rows of kids, heads bent over desks, filling out forms. I wait there, listening and catching my breath.

"Clayton, Pat," the teacher's saying.

"Here."

"Compton, Ellen."

"Here."

"Compton, Richard."

"Here."

All I have to do is open the door.

"Crocker, Alexandra." Nobody calls me Alexandra. "Crocker, Alexandra."

I turn the knob.

"Crossfield, Adam."

"Here."

I open the door, expecting it to be heavy, like the double doors I'm so used to, but it's not. It's light and it flies on its hinges, hitting the wall behind with a bang. Everybody jumps, including the teacher, and I cross my arms and tilt my head, hoping to cover up how freaked out I feel.

"Hi," I say. I picture Stacy the first time I ever laid eyes on her, standing so tough with her hands on her hips. Filled with secrets that none of us could see through all that attitude. "I'm Crocker, Alexandra." I imagine how scared and brave she must have felt, both at the same time, and imagining that helps me smile my best smile. "So," I say, "let's get this party started."

Postscript

Dear Simon,

I'm sorry this letter took me so long. I wrote so many, but none of them sounded the way I wanted them to. I understand a lot of things now that I didd't before. One of those things is that when you have something really important to say, it's practically impossible to say it the right way. The other thing is that the older you get, the more confusing everything else gets. Did you know that? I don't know if you know this, either, but the reason why Stacy lied about you was because her father was touching her and doing sexual stuff with her. My dad says that Stacy was scared and that she might have felt safer telling people that it was you who did all that than saying it was her own father. I think that's a messed-up, mean thing to lie about, but my dad says that when kids are being hurt badly, they sometimes do messed-up, mean things and that you probably know that and probably would forgive her. I guess the thing that's harder for me is that nobody was doing that stuff to me, but I got confused anyway, and I guess (I hate to admit this, but you already know), I guess I started wondering if you had done or wanted to do things to me. After everything happened and you left, I tried to imagine what it would be like if Tim ever accused me of doing something terrible, like setting a dog on fire or beating up a really little kid in the lower school, and what it would be like if he really believed it and if he got other people to believe it too. I could barely even imagine what that would feel like, but even just thinking about it made me want to throw up. I'm serious. I guess that's how you must have felt when we were in Maggie's office with that detective and at other times, too. Like throwing up. So I wanted to write that I'm sorry, and I am sorry, but it feels so stupid to write those words and expect that would make things better for you. "I'm sorry" is so lame, after what's happened, and I know that. You are the best teacher, ever, and you taught me so much stuff about school things and about life things too. I feel so bad because I wasn't smart enough to know that you'd never hurt anyone, especially not a kid. I know that you wouldn't, Simon, and I'm so so so so so so sorry that I doubted all that before, when it mattered so much. If you don't feel like writing me back, I'll understand. Tim really likes your letters, even if his letters back to you sound like he doesn't care (he lets me read what he writes sometimes—I hope that's okay), so please keep writing to him. I guess you know he's going to St. John's next year, and I'm going to Lincoln. Nobody knows where Stacy is, but my dad still calls that detective for any news. My parents are not happy that this letter took me so long to write, and they say to tell you they send their best wishes and to call them anytime. Well, I guess that's all for now. I'll never, ever forget you.

Love, Alex

P.S.

Maybe someday we could run down a mountain again together.

P.P.S.

If you'd rather not, that's okay.

P.P.P.S.

Remember when you taught us what P.S. means?

Acknowledgments

The author gratefully acknowledges and warmly thanks:

Jessica Roland, for a decade of invaluable encouragement and for heroic readings of multiple versions.

Kathy Farrow, for two drafts' worth of feedback, as well as for being there from the start and calling out on the subway so many years later.

Stephen Lucas, for his steadfast mind and heart and for wisely suggesting a different ending.

Karin Cook, Kerry Garfinkel, Stacy Liss, and Amy Rosenblum, for their ongoing support and editorial assistance.

Bunny Gabel, her 1996–97 students, and the Virginia Center for Creative Arts, for providing the space.

Charlotte Sheedy, for wanting it from the absolute beginning.

Richard Jackson, for always.

David, Rebecca, and Ilana, just because.

Turn the page for a preview of
E. R. Frank's gritty new novel, *Dime*.

WHEN I FIRST understood what I was going to do, I expected to write the note as Lollipop. But in the six weeks since then, I've had to face facts. Lollipop has lived in front of one screen or another her whole life, possesses the vocabulary of a four-year-old, can't read, and thinks a cheeseburger and a new pair of glitter panties are things to get excited about. Using her is just a poor idea.

Back in August, Daddy assigned Lollipop to me, saying, *You school her.* I must have been doing a good job hiding my insides from him, or he wouldn't have. L.A. was still the only one of us who was allowed to touch the money. If she found out, it would be the second time she'd learn about Daddy asking me to hold coins. Which would only make things worse than they already were.

Lollipop didn't know the difference between a twenty and a one. "What's that?" She held out her hands, nails trimmed neatly and painted little-girl pink. She was polite, even if she was stupid. "May I touch it, please?"

"Nobody touches the money but Daddy."

"Listen to you," Brandy said from the couch where she was dabbing Polysporin on the cut over her eye that was taking so long to heal. "Cat gave back your tongue?"

"You're touching the money now," Lollipop said. She leaned her head in close to get the best look she could. Then she sniffed. At the one first. Then the twenty. "It stinks."

"Stop," I told her. "Money is dirty. You don't know where it's been. Don't put your nose on it."

Brandy grunted. "That there the funniest thing I heard all week." She didn't sound amused.

I pointed. "That's a two." I pointed again. "That's a zero. That's twenty."

"I know that says twenty." Lollipop pretended to be offended. She was obviously lying. "What's that one?"

"A one next to a zero is ten. You didn't even learn any of this from TV?"

"They have numbers on *Sesame Street* all the time," Lollipop said. "And *Little Einsteins*. *Mickey Mouse Clubhouse*. They have it on a bunch of stuff. So I know them, but I never paid attention to what's more. Only I know a hundred is a lot and a thousand is even more than that. A thousand keeps me pretty in pink."

"Do you know letters?" I asked.

Lollipop nodded. "Yeah," she said. "TV and Uncle Ray taught me those."

Brandy grunted again. "I bet he did."

"Do you know how to read?"

"Some signs." Lollipop scrunched up her face, thinking. *"Exit."*

I waited.

"*Ladies.* Um. *Ice.*"

I waited some more.

"Maybe that's all the signs I know. But I can read two books."

That didn't seem likely. "Which ones?"

"'In the great green room, there was a telephone and a red balloon . . .'"

Some kind of a hiss or a gasp or the sound of a punctured lung came out of Brandy.

"'. . . and a picture of the cow jumping over the moon.'"

Brandy flew off the couch as much as anybody still limping can and smacked Lollipop so hard that Lollipop fell, a perfect handprint seeping onto her cheek. She didn't cry out a sound.

Not a whimper, not a squeak. She just got still, like a statue knocked over. You have to respect an eleven-year-old who gets smacked like that for no good reason and keeps quiet. That Uncle Ray trained her well.

"Brandy!" I stepped between the two of them. Brandy wasn't weak, but this. This was a whole side of her I never knew existed.

Her face was twisted up again the way it had been the other day with Daddy, only now it was beat up from him, fat lip and bruised eyes.

"What was that?" Brandy asked Lollipop. Her cut seeped blood right through the shiny Polysporin. "What was that?"

Lollipop answered as plain as she could manage. She didn't move any part of herself but her mouth. "*Goodnight Moon.*"

"Get off the floor."

"Brandy." Those flames that were lit in my belly the day we took Lollipop rose up, flaring. Was Brandy going to turn vicious now, on top of everything with Daddy? But Lollipop was standing, calm as anything.

"Don't you ever say those words again." Brandy smacked Lollipop's other cheek. Lollipop went down. This time tears oozed like rain dribbling down a wall.

"Daddy's going to kill you," I told Brandy. Even saying

Daddy made me want to slide through the floor and die, but there was nowhere to slide to and no way to die, so somehow I just kept on.

Brandy slipped around the corner to the alcove where my sleeping bag was. I heard her zipping into it. *L.A.'s going to kill you!* I wanted to shout, but the cat took back my tongue again. Anyway, probably Daddy was getting home before L.A., who was doing an outcall. So Daddy would get to Brandy first.

I hauled Lollipop up and propped her on the couch. I made sure the bills we had been studying were in my back pocket. Then I wrapped ice in a paper towel and held it to both sides of her face. She had white features and good, light-brown hair. Her skin was the color of wet sand. Mostly she seemed white, but with that color, it was confusing. She was prettier than the rest of us. Baby-faced.

"What's the other book you know?" I asked her. "Whisper." I didn't want Brandy hearing anything else that might make her charge back out here. But it had been a long time since anybody could talk to me about any kind of book.

"'Be still,'" Lollipop whispered. "It's monsters. There's more, but I can't remember it right now."

Somebody who smelled like barbecue potato chips used to cuddle me on her lap and read to me. I didn't remember the reader; just that salty, smoky scent and something scratchy on my left shoulder every time a page was turned. I remembered the books, though: *Goodnight Moon* and *The Snowy Day*.

"'A wild ruckus,'" Lollipop tried.

"Rumpus." I used to love *Where the Wild Things Are*.

E. R. FRANK

is the author of four novels. Her second book, *America*, was made into a made-for-television movie. In addition to being a writer, she is also a psychotherapist with a specialty in trauma. She has earned a postgraduate certificate from New York's Institute for Contemporary Psychotherapy and is a consultant in Eye Movement Desensitization and Reprocessing (EMDR) therapy. E. R. Frank is a member of the Child Welfare League of America's national advisory board and is also an advisory board member of New York City's Behind the Book. After many years of living in Brooklyn and Manhattan, she has settled in New Jersey with her husband and two children. You can visit her at erfrank.com.

Discover the gritty world of acclaimed author E. R. FRANK.

★"AN IMPORTANT WORK."—*School Library Journal* on ***Dime***, STARRED REVIEW

★"A WRENCHING TOUR DE FORCE."—*Kirkus Reviews* on ***America***, STARRED REVIEW

★"GRIPPING . . . UNSETTLING."—*Booklist* on ***Friction***, STARRED REVIEW

"COMPULSIVELY READABLE."—*School Library Journal* on ***Wrecked***

CRANK

"The poems are masterpieces of word, shape, and pacing . . . stunning."
—*SLJ*

GLASS

"Powerful, heart-wrenching, and all too real."
—*Teensreadtoo.com*

FALLOUT

"*Fallout* is impossible to put down."
—*VOYA*

BURNED

"Troubling but beautifully written."
—*Booklist*

SMOKE

"A strong, painful, and tender piece."
—*Kirkus Reviews*

IMPULSE

"A fast, jagged, hypnotic read."
—*Kirkus Reviews*

PERFECT

"This page-turner pulls no emotional punches."
—*Kirkus Reviews*

IDENTICAL

★"Sharp and stunning . . . brilliant."
—*Kirkus Reviews*, starred review

TRICKS

"Distinct and unmistakable."
—*Kirkus Reviews*

TILT

"Graphic, bitingly honest, and volumious verse."—*SLJ*

RUMBLE

"Strong and worthy."
—*Kirkus Reviews*

PRINT AND EBOOK EDITIONS AVAILABLE